ABANDONED

by Jeri Massi

PEABODY
ADVENTURE SERIES

Bob Jones University Press, Greenville, South Carolina 29614

ABANDONED

Edited by Gary Balius

Cover by Tom Halverson
Illustrations by Dana Thompson

©1989 by Bob Jones University Press
Greenville, South Carolina 29614

ISBN 0-89084-467-4

Printed in the United States of America

20   19   18   17   16   15   14   13   12   11   10   9   8   7

My sincere thanks to Robyn, whose insight, advice, and information helped hold the project together.

This book is dedicated to Cherie Blessing, whose hospitality opened many doors for me up in the *real* New England.

Books by Jeri Massi

The Bracken Trilogy

The Bridge
Crown and Jewel
The Two Collars

The Peabody Series

Derwood, Inc.
A Dangerous Game
Treasure in the Yukon
Courage by Darkness
Llamas on the Loose
Abandoned

Publisher's Note

The Peabody Series presents the adventures of a group of Christian young people from the First Bible Church of Peabody, Wisconsin. Each book focuses on a new adventure that involves several members of the youth group. The characters in these books do not find quick solutions to their difficulties. Like all Christians, they struggle to grow, sometimes losing ground but ultimately coming to a deeper knowledge of the Lord.

This story is narrated by Jack, who tells what happens after the Derwoods, Scruggs, and Annette are left stranded in the mountains of New England. In spite of the fighting and arguing that ensues, the group learns to look to the Lord for strength and grace, managing to work together and to survive. For Jack, the adventure opens up a whole new experience in understanding and liking other people—even people like Annette.

Contents

Chapter One

Off the Ground

Penny was in charge of getting us to Uncle Bill's motel, which is why I can only give a sketchy account of where we were when everything happened. Penny could be more exact about the airport, but of course after that she wouldn't be able to be more exact than me. But as for me, I'm not even sure where the airport was. Once you get out of Boston, you're flying over "the real New England." That's what everyone on the plane kept saying.

We'd be looking down at mountains, and someone would say, "Yup, that's the *real* New England!" as though Boston had only been a cleverly contrived fake or some type of tourist trap that snapped up the unwary. And a stewardess, walking by, would nod and say, "Yup, it's the real New England. Don't see foliage like that anywhere else, do you?"

The tiny plane we'd picked up in Boston was a commuter. Just think of a sardine can with wings, propelled by rubber bands, and you'll get the idea. Scruggs, needless to say, was sick. He hadn't wanted to come in the first place, but I'd talked him into it, and my Uncle Bill had called him up to ask him

1

especially. Scruggs had met my Uncle Bill about a year before.

Jean, though not sick, was really pale. She'd held out fine as long as we'd been riding in something nice and big like a 727, but the commuter flight kept reminding her that she was hanging between earth and sky with no visible means of support.

Penny, as usual, was in control of everything including herself. She was sitting next to Annette, which didn't make her very happy, and Jean was in the aisle seat, hugging the armrests and looking across me to Scruggs, who had his head in his hands.

As for me, I was really happy. I'd saved up all my money since who-knows-when and had made one of those once-in-a-lifetime purchases that everyone *ooohs* and *aahs* over: a 35-millimeter camera. And now we were going to the very farthest part of New Hampshire, and I was planning on getting shots of the mountains, shots of deer, and shots of moose. I had every kind of lens imaginable in my big camera case.

"Jack, I wish you'd quit swinging that camera case around," Penny said.

"Shhh," Scruggs said with a moan. He dropped his head back onto his knees.

"It's getting in the flight attendant's way," she added in a whisper. I made a face at her, but I quit swinging the case. Penny's all right, but having to sit next to Annette had put her into a really bad mood, and whenever she gets into a bad mood, she pulls out her big-sister routine and bosses everyone around.

I had the camera around my neck because I wanted to look like a tourist. Everyone else on the plane did, and I wanted to blend in and act natural.

"Jack's so immature," Annette added.

I challenged her. "Define maturity. I've got a 35-millimeter camera, and you don't."

"Would you please be quiet?" Scruggs moaned again. "When is this flight going to end?"

The plane's interior was dark, but we had the little lamps over our seats turned on. Penny glanced at her watch. "Twenty-four more minutes," she said. "Then we pick up the airport's van, and it takes us to Littleton."

"How long does that take?" I asked.

"Uncle Bill said it could take as long as two and a half hours if lots of people get on with us," she said. "He said normally it takes about an hour and a half."

The plane suddenly jolted.

Scruggs sprang to life. "What was that?" he yelled. "What was that!"

"Wind," I told him.

He glanced at me and then put his head back into his hands. "Oh." And then he mumbled, mostly to himself, "What am I doing here?"

I think that everybody other than Penny and me was asking that question. Penny and I have been out to see my Uncle Bill before—in San Francisco. He doesn't have any children, and he really likes having us visit him. But his latest invitation, which had at first been extended to Penny and me alone, had suddenly, and warmly, included Jean as being of age. And then we'd found out that he'd invited Scruggs to come up to see him, too. And somehow at the last minute my mom had told us that Annette was coming, too.

ABANDONED

Perhaps, if you know much about Penny and me, you know about Annette. She's a year younger than Penny and is kind of always trying to get up to Penny's level, if you know what I mean.

Annette always knows her verses in Sunday school (so does Penny, but for different reasons, I think), and she always knows who *doesn't* know his verses. Overall, she's the kind of kid who reminds the teacher to collect the homework. She used to really run Jean, who's kind of meek, and she still bosses Jean around a lot, if we let her. But mostly she'd set her sights on Penny, trying to get Penny to like her and trying to act like she and Penny were really the best of friends, although they hid it well.

Well, anyway, not one of us had given a thought to having Annette come along. But suddenly she was one of us. And it hadn't been much fun so far, because she really couldn't stand Scruggs.

The plane at last tilted to one side, leveled again, and began its descent. Scruggs gave a shuddering sigh. Jean remained rigid.

I'd gotten a lot of gadgets to go with my camera, and so I fished out my infrared flash. I fixed it onto the camera so that I'd be ready as soon as we got off the plane, I wanted to get a picture of it at night. The plane against the dark mountains.

"Is your seat belt on, Jack?" Annette asked.

"Cool it, Annette," I said. Penny was on a kick to be nice to Annette, but I wasn't. If she was going to come along, she was going to learn not to boss me around. Annette whispered something to Penny, and Penny grunted in answer. Penny wasn't very happy about this adventure, and I felt unsure. I wasn't sure even then if it was going to be fun or not.

As it turned out, it was a lot more fun, and a lot more awful, than anything I'd ever been through before.

Chapter Two
In a Fix

It was pretty dark when we got off the plane. The airport was what I would call Advanced Stone Age: a glassed-in hallway with a small control tower. The flight crew simply carted all the luggage that was inside the plane out onto the side of the taxiing area, and piled it up there for the passengers to sort out and take away.

"I wish Uncle Bill could have come to get us," Jean said. She'd never flown anywhere before, and I could see that she felt a little lost.

"He wanted to, but that case he's on has got him all tied up," Penny said. "Don't worry. He'll take care of us. He called ahead about the airport van and made sure it was all right—Jack, what are you doing? It's too dark for pictures!"

"Not with my infrared flash!" I sighted toward the plane, focused as best as I could, and took the picture. "There!" I exclaimed. "Welcome to New Hampshire!"

"Vermont," Scruggs reminded me. He seemed to be feeling better now that the flight was over. "We're still in Vermont. We'll cross into New Hampshire in the van."

"Developing pictures costs money," Annette scolded. "What's the use of taking pictures of the dark?"

"A lot you know," I began.

"Whoa!" Penny yelled. "Let's get our stuff and get the van. Then you can argue as much as you want."

"We weren't arguing," I said.

"Come on, Jack," Scruggs added. "Let's get our stuff."

Most of the people had been commuters without much luggage, and by now they were all drifting toward the so-called terminal. As we were gathering up our suitcases and knapsacks, a van came bouncing over a narrow service road and drove up alongside the plane.

"You the airport van?" Penny asked.

"Sure." The driver leaned his head out of the window. "Lotta' stuff there. You moving up here?"

Penny grimaced. "No, it's just a visit. We're here to see our uncle."

"I'll get out and give you a hand."

He helped us load our stuff into the van. As we were doing that, Jean said, "Oh look, there goes another van out there onto the highway. I didn't know this place got so many people to use so many vans."

"Oh sure," he said cheerfully. "Vermont's a nice tourist stop. It's real New England, if you know what I mean."

"By now we do," I mumbled.

"Lotta' folks come up here just to hunt," he added. "Or hike. They take transport out to their favorite hideaway and foot it from there on until they go back home." He slammed the back doors shut. "Hop in."

"Do you know how to get to where we're going?" Penny asked. "It's all the way in Littleton, but my uncle said he called."

The driver nodded as he walked around to his side of the van. "Sure. That's no problem. I've carted folks farther than that. Which cabin is he staying in?"

He meant motel cabins. Penny told him, and we all climbed in.

In the darkness of the van I took off the infrared flash and put it back in the case, but I left the camera hanging around my neck.

We were all dog-tired. There were four long seats in the back. Scruggs and I shared one, and we let the girls each take one apiece.

"What brings you up here this time of year?" the driver asked. "An't you got school?"

"Teachers' in-service," Penny told him. "That lasts three days, and the principal let us take two more as long as we made up the work."

"We're all honor roll students," Annette added. Then she glanced at Scruggs. "Almost all, anyway."

He opened one eye and grinned at her without saying anything. She gave a little flounce of her shoulders and turned forward in her seat.

The ride took a long, long time. Penny asked the guy once if we were almost there. There was nothing to look at in the darkness. The van was winding its way through the White Mountains.

" 'Bout halfway," he told her. "These old vans don't make such good time, but they get you there."

Scruggs was already asleep, and so was Jean. I felt sure that Penny would stay awake, so I fell asleep, too.

ABANDONED

The last thing that I remember was the pleasant jolting of the van on the highway, and feeling a little too warm because all the windows were closed. A long time later, I realized that everything was very still. I opened my eyes and saw that the sun was coming up. Up over mountains that were tipped with snow. It was beautiful, and I remembered that we were in New England (the *real* New England) for a week with Uncle Bill. Then I realized that we were still in the van, and that it was cold.

I sat up and looked around. Penny, Annette, Scruggs, Jean—they were all sprawled in their seats, asleep. The driver was gone. The van was silent. We were out in the woods somewhere, and there was no road, only a double-rutted trail.

"Hey!" I exclaimed. "Hey! Penny! Scruggs! We've been left somewhere!"

Scruggs sleepily lifted up his head, cringing from a cramp in his neck. "What?" he asked.

I bolted to the side door and pulled it open, then jumped down outside the van. The air was chill and crisp. It was early November. That was the first thought that hit me—we might not be dressed warmly enough for the weather.

I looked around. The van had been left in a fairly high place. I could see other ridges of mountains. The trees were bare of leaves.

Scruggs and Penny came tumbling out of the van.

"Oh no!" Penny exclaimed.

"But why would he do it?" Scruggs asked. "Maybe something went wrong. Maybe he left us a note on the driver's seat."

He ran around to the front of the van and looked inside. "No," he called back to us. More bewildered, Annette and Jean followed out of the van. They looked around.

"Where are we?" Jean asked.

"I don't know," Penny said. She looked at me, and understanding slowly dawned on us both. We must have been driving for hours through the White Mountains. The guy had driven the van until all the gas was gone and we were all asleep.

"We could be anywhere," I said.

"Quiet," Scruggs ordered. He wasn't mad, just stern. He looked at me, and I got the message. This was no time to get scared. "Listen," he said after a minute, "we've been left. We're in trouble. But the only way to get out of trouble is to make a plan and follow it."

Jean and Penny nodded at his words. "We've been left," he said again. "Somebody means no good, and I think he might come back. So we've got to get out of sight of the van, at least to where we can safely plan what to do."

"We could get lost if we try to leave this place," Penny said.

"It might be more dangerous to stay," Scruggs added. "But let's at least get out of sight—with enough stuff to make a getaway if we have to."

Chapter Three
Making a Plan

We clambered into the back of the van for our luggage. Some of it had been left, but some had been taken. My camera case was gone, and so was Penny's. She'd only brought along a little Instamatic in a hand-held case, but it had been taken.

"Well," I said, when I realized that my lenses had been stolen. "They got everything else, but if they come back, they're not getting my camera. I'm glad I had it hung around my neck."

"It may turn out to be nothing but extra weight, Jack," Scruggs told me.

"I said I'm taking it," I told him.

We had brought along a lot of trail clothing, and most of that was left.

"Layer the shirts," Scruggs told us.

"All our knapsacks are gone," Jean lamented.

"Not mine," Annette said. "I was using it as a pillow. Here it is."

"Good," Scruggs said. "I brought along five flannel shirts. Everybody can use one. We'll stow them, first of all." He glanced at Jean's luggage. "If we run into really bad weather, you'll need something stouter than what you've got in there."

"The knapsack is *mine!*" Annette exclaimed. "I'll decide what goes into it!"

Scruggs looked at her. Penny did, too—both of them real sudden, and—for once—real silent.

"Look," I said, trying to lighten things. "We've all got to be a team, right? Share and share alike. If Scruggs wants to share his shirts, we all ought to share what we've got."

"I don't want one of his smelly shirts," Annette said. "That's disgusting."

"All right," Scruggs said. "The knapsack is yours. But when it comes time to share food, and maybe safety, and other things we haven't even thought of—maybe then we'll start deciding what belongs to us and not to you."

I think that for the first time she got the idea of what kind of fix we were in. And more than that, she realized that all of us, not just Scruggs, wanted her to share the knapsack. She flung it down. "Oh, all right. I just don't like being bossed around. You could have asked, Scruggs Grady."

He didn't answer her, just stuffed all five folded up shirts into the knapsack. "Socks," he said next. "No, better yet, we'll stuff our pockets with them." He looked up. "Have we got anything to eat?"

We were all starving, now that the first shock was wearing off. We'd been on three connecting flights to get to Vermont, and on each one we'd gotten what they call "a snack." Nobody had wanted the smoked almonds that the stewardesses passed out.

"If only we'd saved those almonds!" I exclaimed.

"I did," Penny told me. She started to pull them out of various pockets. "I love those things, and I thought we might all feel differently about them once we got onto the van at the airport."

"Mom sent that box along to Uncle Bill," I said, foraging through the pile of stuff. "It's cheese."

"I've got candy in my suitcase," Jean said.

"Me too," I added.

All told we had about ten of those tiny packets of smoked almonds, a five-pound cheese, a link of salami, six candy bars, a box of cough drops, and two bags of chocolate drops.

"This isn't very much," Scruggs said.

"Matches," Penny said. "Who's got matches?"

He looked at her. "You're right. We'll never get anywhere without them."

But none of us had any.

Jean ran to the front of the van and clambered in on the passenger side. "There's some in the glove compartment!" she exclaimed. She brought back two boxes and handed them to Scruggs. He smiled at her. "Good thinking," he told her. "This outfit needs some brains like yours."

Annette glowered at that, whether because Jean had so trustingly handed all of our matches to Scruggs or because he'd been so plain to compliment her, I don't know.

"Heaviest shoes and heaviest jackets," he said. "Then let's get all the other shirts that we can into the knapsack or tied 'round our waists."

We did as he said. The last thing that he did was to pull out his slim pocket Bible from his suitcase. He slid it into his jacket pocket.

ABANDONED

"Let's backtrack along this road," he said. "Or path, or whatever it is. We'll pick out a good hiding place and make our plans. No talking as we walk. Keep your ears open for some sound of anybody else around."

Or anything, I told myself. Suddenly the prospects of sighting bear and moose weren't quite as much fun as they had been last night.

Chapter Four
Taking a Vote

We walked about a quarter mile down the double-rutted path before we picked a sheltered place to clamber into. By that time we were pretty well warmed up, although the air was crisp and our breath was hanging like smoke in front of our faces.

"I have seven o'clock," Scruggs said. "At the longest, we could have been traveling in the van until four or five in the morning. It was about eight o'clock when we drove out of the airport."

"We could be three or four hundred miles from the airport," Penny said. "We could be anywhere."

"Well, we're still in the mountains," he said.

"Maybe we're somewhere up in Canada," I guessed. "Or Maine."

"The thing is," Penny added, "he only had to get us about fifty or sixty miles away from everybody to make sure that—that—"

"Say it," Scruggs said. "Let's say the worst and face it now."

"To make sure that we'd never get back."

"Is it that bad?" Jean asked.

"You're all crazy," Annette said. "The van broke down, and he went to get help, that's all."

"He would have told us," Scruggs said. "Or left a note or something."

"Scruggs is right," I added. "He drove around until we were all sound asleep. Then he took our stuff and left."

"But he had to go somewhere," Jean said. "How did he walk away with all our stuff—our knapsacks and camera cases?"

"Maybe somebody met him up here," Penny guessed. "Like, right before he picked us up, he arranged with someone to meet near here, and that person drove him away."

"If that's true," Scruggs said, "we can hope that this place is somewhat local—a spot that both people were familiar with. We may not be as far from help as I've been thinking."

"What I want to know is why," I said. "Why do something that rotten?"

"That's what scares me," Scruggs said.

"What do you mean?" I asked.

"For some reason, right on the spur of the moment, maybe, that guy posed as a van driver. He didn't have time to do anything else but take us up here to the middle of nowhere and leave us. But now he has time. He might come back with a better plan in mind. Better to him."

"We've got to get out of here," Jean said.

"It's crazy to go walking through the wilderness like this," Penny said.

Taking a Vote

"It would be crazier to stay," he said. "We don't know who our friends are, but we do know we've got an enemy. And right now, he knows where we are."

"If you get lost in the woods you're supposed to stay in one place," she insisted.

"Penny, I know that," he told her. "But that guy's likely put us where he's sure a search party won't even think of finding us. Don't you understand? We're lost from all the good guys—we've got to get lost from all the bad guys, too."

"I'm with Scruggs," I said. "If we'd gotten ourselves lost, I'd say to stay put and concentrate on making help signals. But with things as they are, I think we need to get out of here."

"Me too," Jean said. "If we don't just walk in circles, we ought to reach some kind of town or something eventually."

"As long as we can keep walking," Scruggs said. He didn't add anything to that, but I knew what he was thinking. How long could we keep walking with almost no food and no weapons?

"I'm not going anywhere," Annette said. "I think you're all crazy."

"You'll go all right," Scruggs said. "As soon as we leave you alone in the woods for five minutes you'll be begging us to wait up for you."

"Penny and I are staying!" she snapped. "You can do what you like. And the knapsack is mine!"

Penny shook her head. "No. I'm going if they go. We'll only make it if we work together. I think we should stay, but if the vote is to go, I'll go."

Annette folded her arms and wouldn't say anymore.

"But," Penny added, "if we go, where do we go?"

ABANDONED

"We ought to pick one direction and stick with it," I said.

"That would be nice," Scruggs told me. "But probably impossible. The land itself might block us. What if we should come to a river?"

Penny sat back on her heels. "Look," she said. "If that guy really wanted to get us lost, then he took us north of Littleton, whether thirty miles or three hundred. So we ought to at least try to go in a southerly direction, even if we have to make detours. Don't you have a compass, Jack?"

"It was in my knapsack," I told her.

"I've got one," Scruggs said. "That path that he drove up goes back toward the south—at least so far as I can tell. We ought to follow it."

"Maybe it will lead back to the highway," Jean added.

"Maybe," Scruggs added. "But most likely it will join other trails. If he really intended to lose us, then he's probably set us far from any roads."

"Even trails lead somewhere," Jean said.

"True," he agreed. "And the sooner we start out, the sooner we'll know." He stood up. "I think we ought not to talk as we go along—at least not for a while. Let's keep alert for sounds of people or cars—or water," he added.

"What about breakfast?" Annette began, but then Penny said, "Wait a second!"

We all looked at her. "What?" Scruggs asked.

"I think we'd better vote on a few things," she suggested.

Scruggs looked guarded. "Like what?"

"Like getting along and deciding on things," she told him. "We won't get far if we argue the whole way."

"Penny's right," Annette said. She smirked at Scruggs.

"Nobody asked you, Annette!" I exclaimed. "You wouldn't even share your knapsack!"

"Jack!" Scruggs exclaimed, and Penny echoed him. I shut my mouth, but I was mad. Annette was going to do everything she could to make Scruggs look bad. Why in the world did she have to come with us?

"All right," Scruggs said. "Let's vote on things, then." He sat back down.

"We ought to pick a leader," Penny said. He nodded.

"Penny for leader," Annette said. I bit down on my teeth.

Penny shook her head. "Scruggs for leader. He's oldest and strongest."

Scruggs was startled by her nomination. He'd really been leading us since we'd gotten up, and I knew Scruggs well enough to know that he thought himself the only one really able to get us anywhere. But all the same, he was surprised to see Penny agreeing so loyally with him. So was I.

Penny can be bossy sometimes, but she's sure level-headed when things get tough. I guess I'd never thought much about that until then.

"I vote for Scruggs, too," I said, and Jean nodded. "Me too."

We all looked at Annette. She just looked away, really mad again.

"As far as food," Scruggs said, "let's try to get along without breakfast—at least for a while. We've got to make what we've got last."

ABANDONED

He didn't look at any of us as he said it. I knew what he was thinking—a five-pound cheese and a salami between five people might last two days. And even stretching it that far was going to take a lot of will power. But if it lasted that far—then what?

Chapter Five

Something Useful

It was close to eight o'clock before we got everything settled and could start out. The trail took us down the mountain, but it was a long walk. On our way down we did pass one huge open field of grass, and Scruggs halted long enough to scan the whole area for signs of a house or barn or something, but there was nothing.

The trees around us were nearly bare, except for the evergreens, of course, and there were more of those as we walked along. These weren't the kinds of woods that Penny and I had seen in Pennsylvania: the trees we'd seen there had been mostly aspens and birches and young beech trees. This forest felt older and bigger somehow.

As we came closer to the foot of the mountain, the woods grew closer and closer to the trail, until they crowded over us. By that time we were all getting tired, especially Jean, who was lagging behind. Mom had gotten her new hiking shoes for the trip, and Jean had put them on when Scruggs ordered us to take our sturdiest shoes. But already she was limping in them. That's Jean. If anything can go wrong, it usually does, and it usually happens to Jean.

"You got blisters?" I asked, dropping behind to walk with her. She nodded without answering. Scruggs was pretty athletic, and Penny and I had always liked hiking and exploring. But Annette wasn't much at sports or anything and didn't strike me as being very strong. And Jean was the youngest and smallest of us by far. She was eleven, and there wasn't much to her. She wiped the sweat off her face and put her glasses back on.

"Let me take some of your stuff," I said. She had a sweatshirt tied by its sleeves around her waist, which she handed to me, and she was wearing her waterproof windbreaker under her jacket. She got the windbreaker off and handed that to me, too. But we'd gone only about two miles, and I knew she was going to have to rest soon. This was going to be a hard day for her.

"There's a clearing up ahead," Scruggs called back to us.

He was right. The forest along the trail had gotten much more dense, but through the trees ahead we could see blue sky. The trail itself veered off into the trees, running parallel to the wide empty space.

"Let's cut through and see what's out there," Scruggs said.

Even Jean perked up with curiosity. We forced our way through the tangled underbrush and broke out into the open. Scruggs came out first and stopped, speechless with amazement. Penny came out next and then I came out with Jean and Annette. We all stopped and stared.

A wide swath had been cut right through the forest, like a giant's road. All that was left were stumps, cut close to the ground. The swath must have been as wide as two city blocks, and it ran across the slope, dipped out of sight, and continued on up another slope and back up the mountain. For some reason the sight of that desolate strip, running out of sight up the mountain, made everything seem much more vast and empty than it had before. We were all speechless, until at last Scruggs said, "This must have been done fairly recently. There aren't any seedlings or saplings between the stumps. Maybe this past summer."

"But how could somebody do all this?" Jean asked. "It must have taken hundreds of people to cut down all those trees. They must live around here somewhere."

"No," I told her. "Paper mills and lumber companies own a lot of wilderness land up here. They send up machines and a few men to do it. In fact," I added, "I think it means that we really are stranded. I think that these lumbering areas are usually set far away from towns."

"These trails are just the truck roads that the lumberjacks used this past summer," Scruggs said. "They might just lead from camp to camp. We could follow this one around in a big circle!"

It was a pretty bleak moment.

Suddenly Annette spoke up, and she said the first sensible thing that I think I'd ever heard from her. "Even if it leads from camp to camp, as long as it gets us off this mountain, we might find some sign of a permanent road somewhere. Maybe even a road sign or something that the lumbermen put up."

"You're right," Scruggs said. "Let's get back to it." But suddenly he bent down. "Wait a second. Here's something useful." He picked up a grayed axe handle without any head on it.

"What's the use of that?" I asked him.

"Well, it's a good guide stick, for one," he told me. "It's not rotten at all. And for two, we might find a club handy. Come on."

Without another word, we forced our way back through the forest and onto the trail again.

It wasn't nearly noon yet, but after stopping once I found it hard to go on again. I was so hungry that it hurt. We did find a stream farther on, and we all drank from it. That helped a little bit, but not for long. Finally Scruggs stopped and looked back. Jean was far behind from the rest of us. He frowned. I could see he was mad at himself for not thinking of her. Scruggs has gotten pretty uptight with Penny and me in the past for not being nice to Jean, so it was a sore point with him not to have thought about her.

"Why are you limping?" he asked her.

"My shoes are giving me blisters," she said faintly, and sat down right on the ground. We all sat down, one at a time. Even though it was cool outside, we were all sweating.

"It was stupid to bring along so many clothes," Annette said.

"You'll think differently about that tonight," Scruggs told her.

"Oh, stop acting like a know-it-all, Daniel Boone," she snapped.

"Shut up, Annette," I yelled.

Scruggs and Penny both glanced at me. Annette didn't answer, and I didn't add anything, but I wasn't going to apologize to her for saying "shut up." We were

all silent. At last Jean fished out another pair of socks from her pocket and put them on. Scruggs nodded as she laced her shoes up again. "The extra padding may help," he said.

Chapter Six

Vikings on the March

After a rest of about twenty minutes we toiled on again, but it was getting worse for Jean. At last Scruggs gave his pack to Penny to carry, and he bent down for Jean to climb up onto his back.

"I can't," Jean said. "It's not fair for you to have to carry me."

He looked back at her and grinned. "You can pay me back tomorrow and carry me. Come on, get on."

She didn't want to stand there and argue with him, so she gingerly threw her arm around his neck from behind and got astride his back. He straightened up and shrugged her so that her knees were riding over his hips, and we started on again. Piggyback isn't the worst way to carry somebody, once you get into the rhythm of it, but I didn't think Scruggs would be able to keep it up for more than another half hour, even at an easy pace.

Having rested, we relaxed some of our rules and talked as we walked along. Penny dropped back to me, and Annette, of course, dropped back with her.

"You remember that time we had to go to Aunt Irene's and didn't like it?" Penny asked me.

"Sure," I said.

"And we made a deal that we'd pray, remember?" she said.

"Yeah."

"It worked out pretty good, I thought," she said.

I looked at her. "You know, I think so, too." Penny and I never talked about that deal we'd made, but it was true that when we'd stayed at Aunt Irene's, we'd prayed together every night before we went to bed. It was because Mom was in the hospital, and we were homesick, and we didn't like Aunt Irene at first.

But once we'd gotten back home to Peabody, Wisconsin, we'd stopped praying together. All the same, I always had thought that God had heard our prayers— I'd always thought it had been the right thing to pray like we did. And—maybe this sounds strange, or maybe you know what I mean—I can usually pray (like if a teacher calls on me to pray in school) without even thinking, and right after I'm done, I forget all about whatever I said. But some of the prayers we'd prayed at Aunt Irene's still stuck in my head. I had felt close to God at Aunt Irene's, but I didn't always feel that way the rest of the time.

"I think," Penny said, "that we ought to do that again, now."

"You know, I don't think it's right just to pray together when we get into trouble," I told her.

"Well, I try to do it other times, too, Jack!" she exclaimed. (Penny is better at it than I am.) "But," she added, "if it's bad not to pray when everything's okay, it's got to be even worse not to pray when you're in trouble. Maybe God's using the trouble to *teach* us to pray."

"You mean, you two don't know how to pray?" Annette asked.

Now that we were talking about praying, I felt a lot worse about having told Annette to shut up. But I was mad that she'd asked us that. I was sure that Annette didn't know any more about it than we did. Praying's a lot more than just bowing your head and closing your eyes and saying things to God. I know it's more than that. But for some reason I didn't say anything. I wasn't going to argue with Annette about whether or not I could pray. What had happened that summer at Aunt Irene's was too unusual and too happy a memory for me to argue about it. Because, you see, we really had learned to like Aunt Irene, and Penny and I had come out of it better friends than ever before.

Penny glanced at me. "I think we ought to pray when we can—all of us, or at least some of us when we're all together."

"Okay," I said. "I know Scruggs'll go for it."

We trudged on for a short while before Scruggs called a halt again and let Jean slip down from his back.

"We'd better stop," he said. "It's about noon."

Nearby was a small clearing with some fallen logs in it. We went in and sat down, some of us on the logs and some on the ground. After a little discussion about rations, Scruggs cut up the cheese and the salami and passed out some of the candy. I did some arithmetic in my head, estimating a little, and figured it out. What each person got was about four ounces of cheese (a square that would fit on the palm of your hand), a slice of salami, and half of a candy bar. It wasn't enough for anybody, but we felt full for a couple of seconds at least. And at least we had a chance to rest.

Penny stretched out her legs and gave a sigh.

"I know!" Scruggs exclaimed. "You Derwoods are always reading this and reading that and pretending things: let's make believe we're Vikings. Wasn't it Vikings that were the first settlers around here?"

"Somewhere in Canada, I think," Penny ventured. She brightened. "But then, we might be in Canada."

He nodded. "Let's pretend we're from an outpost. We got sent out to see what the Indians were like and to see if there was anything we could trade with them. Now we're on our way back to the main camp because we've heard that another group of Indians raided it."

"No, wait," I said. "Let's pretend that the Indians raided our main camp and took everybody prisoner, so now we've got to find the Indian village. That way it's more like what we're actually doing, trying to find an unknown town."

"Okay, I'll be Leif," Scruggs said. "You be Lars, Jack."

"Lars?" I asked. "No real Viking was ever named Lars!"

"Well, it's a Norwegian name," he told me. "And the girls will be Olga, Helga, and Gertrude."

"No way!" Penny and Annette yelled. Jean burst out laughing.

"We'd better all take real Viking names, girls or no girls," Penny said. "Jack can be Eric if he wants." I nodded.

"Can girls be Vikings?" Jean asked.

"Shield maidens," Scruggs told her with a nod.

"What's a shield maiden?" she asked.

"The unmarried women who could spin and weave and sew and—when things got rough—pick up a sword and shield to defend hearth and hall with the best of them. Back then, self-defense was a family concern. Everyone pitched in," Scruggs said.

"Well, it seems like any woman named Olga or Helga would have to learn to fight," Penny said. "I think I'll take Ooné for my name. Sounds almost like Renée."

"I don't know of any name that I could take," Jean said.

"How about Berwyn?" Penny asked. "I think that's authentic."

Annette wouldn't take a name because she said we were too old for games. So Scruggs called her Grendel whenever we were playing Vikings, but she would never really enter into the spirit of the thing.

Chapter Seven
What and Why

For an hour we rested alongside the trail. Talk turned from Vikings to Uncle Bill. We tried to guess how long it would take him to call the police and try to find us.

"If anybody saw us climb into that van last night, we might have hope," Penny said.

"Only if other people report seeing where the van went," Scruggs told her. "But there weren't many people out on the roads last night. Nobody may have noticed the van at all. Why would they, in the dark, especially?"

He was right. There was nothing suspicious about a van being driven through the mountains. Probably, the few people who'd passed us wouldn't even remember whether they'd seen a van or not.

"And if they do find the van, we won't be anywhere near it," Annette predicted sulkily.

"No, but we'll be easy enough to find," Scruggs told her. "Just follow the trail down from the van for about six miles, and here we are."

"Is that all?" Jean asked. "I thought it was more like fifteen."

He shook his head. "We haven't gone very far."

Penny shook her head as though ashamed and forced a smile. "Viking dropouts," she said.

"The afternoon will be shorter," Scruggs replied. "It gets dark early up here, and we'll have a lot to do to set up our camp."

"Are there bears up here?" Jean asked.

He nodded wearily.

"Scruggs!" Annette said sharply. "Don't scare her!"

I pushed my lips together. Scruggs had closed his eyes, and he didn't bother to open them now. "It was an honest answer," he said. He did open his eyes to look at Jean. "Bears'll stay away from fire. Anyway, that's what I've always heard. And besides, if there have been lumberjacks up here with big machines, most of the bears probably moved to more quiet neighborhoods. They like to get their sleep, too."

"I still keep coming back to why," I said.

"Why what?" Penny asked.

"Why did that guy do it to us?"

She sighed. Scruggs opened his eyes again.

"Maybe it had something to do with those two men by the plane," Jean said at last.

We all looked at her.

"What two men?" Penny asked.

"The one had been on the flight with us, and as we were getting off, the other one ran up to him and they started talking about something. But the first man was mad—or maybe they were both mad. Anyway, then I went to help sort my things out of the luggage pile."

"What would two perfect strangers want from us?" Annette asked, sounding a little annoyed.

Jean shrugged. "I don't know, but they're the only two people there who noticed us at all. They both looked at Jack when he was taking that picture in the dark."

"Anybody would stare at that," Scruggs added with a laugh. "Then what happened?"

"Nothing," she said. "They walked away."

"Doesn't seem like they were all that interested in us," Scruggs said.

I sighed. "Nothing in this mess makes sense."

Penny agreed. "I know. If anybody'd wanted to hurt us or kill us, they could have done it while we were asleep."

"That driver could have slipped the brake off the van and let us roll back down that mountain," Scruggs added.

"Don't!" Jean exclaimed. "That's awful!"

"I'm sorry," he told her. "But you see, it didn't happen."

"It could be happening now," Annette said. "They just let us leave the van, and then they go back and get the van, and everything's just like it was before, except we're gone. And nobody can find us."

We were all silent. It wasn't a nice thought, but it was possible.

"You might be right," Scruggs said at last. "But it's too late to go back, now. We've got to go on." Then, Viking-like, he added, "And if that's the way it's going to be, I'd rather be out here, struggling and going forward, than back at the van, begging whoever kidnaped us to take us back home. I don't like begging."

"Me either," I added. Penny and Jean nodded assent to that, and even Annette didn't argue. It was one o'clock. Scruggs stood up. "Come on, Vikings!" he exclaimed.

ABANDONED

He thrust the axe handle like a sword into his belt. "Our doom is laid upon us. Let us go forward and deem the best course to take to it."

"And what happens when we deem our doom?" I asked him.

He grimaced. "We follow it to the demise of the doom we've deemed, you dodo! Come on!"

Chapter Eight
Setting Up Camp

"There must have been rain lately," Scruggs said as he stooped to examine the ground.

We were off the mountain at last, following a more deeply rutted trail that must have been a main roadway for the lumber trucks. At first the sight of something that seemed like a main drag had cheered all of us. But the trail seemed to do nothing more than wind around the foot of the mountain, and our good mood wore off.

The ground was damp, although none of us had noticed that before.

"Run-off, I guess," Scruggs said. "The ground up on the mountain was drier, but it's still damp down here. This may not be too much fun for getting a fire started. Keep your eyes open for dry branches. We'll have to start collecting them."

Not long after that, I spotted a long, dead branch that had gotten caught in a tangle of other trees. We pulled it down. As Scruggs walked along, he would pick up a single leaf here, and a single leaf there, dry ones that were skipping along the tops of the damp undergrowth on the forest floor.

ABANDONED

The sun seemed to dip down even faster than usual, now that we were needing light to see by. We all wanted to hurry, and I think everybody had an idea of finding a good place to set up a camp. All the same, Scruggs called a halt in order to rest. I guess we all needed it, but especially Jean. We'd been going a lot more slowly than we'd traveled in the morning, but she was having a hard time.

I know I've said before that Jean's the type of person who just attracts misfortunes. But she had a lot of grit. She hadn't complained yet about anything.

Scruggs glanced at her as we sat for a few minutes on the side of the trail.

"Not much further now," he said. "We'll just stop at the first good place we find."

For once, things went our way. Not long after the rest stop, we found a place alongside the trail that had been used as a camp before by somebody else.

"Maybe the men who worked up here had to post a watch over the machinery or something," Scruggs guessed.

"I hear water," Penny said.

He nodded. "So do I, but let's get the fire going first before we go down to find it."

When I stopped to listen, I realized that I could hear it too—a flowing sound. But I couldn't tell where it was coming from.

"Let's scatter and find some firewood if we can," Scruggs ordered. "Nobody go too far. Jean, you stay here. Everybody keep her in sight. That way we won't wander off."

We did as he said. Annette found a dead tree, a slender birch that was hung way over. We pulled off as many branches as we could, and then Scruggs and I grabbed it up near the top and hung on it until a big part of it broke away. We broke it down that way until only an upright chunk of the stump was left. The girls went back to Jean with the wood. Scruggs and I found a fallen tree trunk, but it was too big to move, and we didn't have any tools to cut it up.

All this time, the shadows had been getting longer in the forest. I felt a lot colder. There was no doubt that night was coming fast.

"We need a lot more wood," he said.

We stopped being so picky and just picked up every branch and stick that we found on the forest floor. The girls came back and helped, until at last we had quite a pile of wood in the clearing.

"Some of it's old," Penny said. "But almost all of it's damp."

"I'll show you something," Scruggs said. He took out his penknife and picked up one of the twigs that we'd collected. Using the blade of his knife like a scraper, he peeled up the outer hide of the twig. He kept at it until the twig started to look a little bit like a very hairy hairbrush.

I got the idea. Fluffing out the twigs would make them dry faster and be easier to burn, since air could get through them. I got out my knife and did the same while the light faded.

Meanwhile, Penny directed Annette and Jean to help her strip dry bark from some of the dead wood we'd collected. Penny and I have done a lot of camping, and Scruggs had a lot of plain common sense. He'd also been up into the Yukon before—like I had been—and he remembered a lot of tricks that Jimmy Gray Beaver had showed us when Jimmy had been our guide up in the mountains.

At last we had a good pile of tinder. We cleared a big patch of dirt and piled the tinder up there. Scruggs lit a match. It flared like a tiny torch, and I realized how dark the forest was now. He was careful with the matches. But all the same, it took several of them before the flame caught on the tinder and stayed caught.

None of us dared breathe while he quickly rearranged the bits of bark and leaves so that the tiny flame would survive. He nursed it until it was a respectable tongue of fire. Then he arranged some of our bigger fluffed-out twigs onto it. They sent out a lot of white smoke as the dampness in them evaporated, but they caught fire. We had found a few pine cones, and Scruggs put them on too. At last he added the driest of the branches.

At first a lot of white smoke came out, but it didn't seem to me to take long for the fire to build up. Scruggs arranged the wood on it tepee-style, so that he could just push the sticks up into it as it burned away.

"Now for the water," he said. We all looked up. The forest was dark.

"Maybe we should wait till morning," Jean said.

"I can't," Penny told her. "I'm too thirsty."

"Me too," Annette said.

"Boy, I wish we had a canteen," I said.

"Well, we ought to do it in two shifts," Scruggs said.

"Right," Penny added, "so if one group gets out too far, the group at the fire can halloo them back in."

Annette rolled her eyes. "The water can't be that far."

"Might be far enough," Scruggs said. "Woods in the dark are easy to get lost in—especially if you get a few trees between yourself and the fire."

Penny and Annette and I went down first to find it, and it wasn't very far at all. We could see the fire behind us plain as plain.

"See, I told you," Annette said.

I ignored her as I drank from it and splashed some of the water onto my face.

"Ugh! How can you?" Penny asked. "Your face is going to freeze."

I laughed at her. "It's not that cold yet."

We went back, and then Scruggs and Jean came down for their turn.

The night was cold, though. There was no denying that. We huddled around the fire and waited as Scruggs brought out another part of the cheese and the last of the salami. We got about the same as we'd gotten at lunch, except no candy this time.

"I'm glad for these extra clothes now," Penny said.

We had to sit on some of the shirts we'd brought. We put on the others or draped them over us. But we could all hear things rustling in the trees, and we kept looking back into the darkness.

"You know," Scruggs said. "We never did pray over our dinner."

Penny and I glanced at him.

"Jack and I talked about that earlier," Penny said. "We ought to pray together," she added. She didn't offer any apologies or seem embarrassed.

"You're right," Scruggs said. "What a dope I am. This is just another adventure, after all."

"What's that mean?" Annette demanded.

"It's something Mrs. Bennett told me once," Jean said. "How knights back in the olden days would ask the Lord to send them adventures. And so every time they had one, they knew that it came from the Lord, and they weren't afraid."

"What knights?" she asked. "That doesn't sound like any knights I've ever heard of."

"Well not all of them," Scruggs said. "But it was part of chivalry, and some of the knights really believed it. They called it taking the adventure that the Lord sent them. So ever since Jean told us about it, we've tried to look at it that way."

Penny laughed. "So are we knights, or are we Vikings?"

"Both," I told her.

"We'll sing first," Scruggs said. "And in honor of the water, we'll sing 'Like a River Glorious.'"

So we sang. At first Annette wouldn't join in. I think she thought that we were trying to make fun of her in some way. But the more she looked at the dark woods around us, the more she wanted to sing, so at last she joined in.

Chapter Nine
No Friend of Mine

The singing made us all feel better. We prayed around in a circle. Annette prayed for all the missionaries and the sick people at church, but the rest of us mainly stuck to asking to get out of these woods in one piece. Jean didn't have much to say. I think she felt shy.

Then we had to decide exactly how to spend the night. We were all exhausted, but nobody liked the thought of sleeping unguarded.

"We'll have to split up the night into watches," Scruggs said. "Let's do it two and three—that way nobody has to watch alone. Jack and I will watch first." Penny looked annoyed when he said that, but he added, "Tomorrow night we can all watch with different people."

The girls all huddled into a group to share flannel shirts, which they used as blankets.

"What I wouldn't give for a cup of coffee," Scruggs said in a low voice as the moments ticked away.

"And a doughnut on the side," I added. "Or better yet, Mom's apple pie."

He glanced at me. "Yeah, I'm really hungry, too."

We were silent after that. The girls all dropped off to sleep, and I was nodding from being tired.

"Don't, Jack. We've got to last at least until midnight," Scruggs told me. "It's only nine o'clock."

"Why did that guy do this to us?" I asked.

"Let's not start that again," Scruggs said. "We've got to concentrate on getting out of this."

"Well, we've done okay so far," I said.

He looked at me. "Jack, we've only got food to get through tomorrow—and not too much at that. Then what?"

I looked down. "I don't know. I don't know how anybody could live off the forest without a gun—or at least a bow and arrow."

"Even with a gun," Scruggs said, "there doesn't seem much to shoot at. I haven't seen any squirrels. Have you?"

"No, but we've been making a lot of noise as we've been going, too. If things get worse, we'll learn to be more quiet."

"Quiet or not, we don't even have a gun," Scruggs said.

"Well, we did pray," I reminded him.

"That's good, because if the Lord doesn't do something for us, we're not going to get out of here."

I'd never heard him so low before. "We've been in rougher spots than this, Scruggs," I told him. "And," I added, "the Lord's always gotten us out of them before."

"It would be almost fun if we had food," he said after a pause. "And if Jean's feet weren't bothering her."

"And if Annette had stayed home," I whispered.

He glanced at me and didn't say anything. Annette hated him. That was for sure, but so far Scruggs hadn't given much sign of what he thought of it.

He arranged some more wood on the fire, and it flamed up. Across from us, Jean stirred but stayed asleep. She had taken her shoes off, and her stockinged feet peeped out from under the assorted shirts and jackets that covered them.

We sat and looked at the flames. It was only 9:15. I remembered seeing Scruggs push the sticks up, and then the next thing I knew, a gray and pink dawn was breaking overhead above the trees, and I could hear some kind of rustling in the leaves around us. A cold and wet dew lay over everything. The fire had gone mostly to coals. I was numb everywhere, and hungry on the inside.

I sat up. Everything hurt—mostly because I'd fallen asleep while sitting Indian-style. I groaned and stretched my back. The girls were still asleep in a huddle. Next to me, Scruggs was also Indian-style, with his head propped on his hand, and his hand propped on his knee. His mouth was open.

My breath hung like a cloud in the air. It felt much colder than it had felt the morning before.

"Scruggs," I whispered. He jerked awake. Then he winced and stifled a groan. I staggered to my feet and found the last of the wood. While he untangled himself, I set it on the fire. There was dew on it, but the sticks that had been on the inside of the pile were pretty dry. I put them on first. Then I pushed up the charred ends of last night's fuel. The flames rekindled and grew.

Scruggs stood up and staggered to the edge of the clearing to get the feeling back into his legs.

"We fell asleep," he said, his voice still thick from sleep.

"Yeah," I said. I didn't care. Nothing bad had happened. I put on the last sticks. The girls stirred.

Penny groaned. "Oh, I hate sleeping on the ground!"

I glanced at Scruggs and gave a wry grin. At least she had been lying down.

Jean sat up on her elbows. "Didn't you guys try to wake me up for my turn?" she asked. "I would have watched with you."

"Nobody woke me up," Penny said to her. She glanced at Annette and gave her a nudge. "Wake up, Annette!"

"Get out!" Annette's voice said.

"Come on, it's morning!" Penny exclaimed. "There's a bear up the trail."

Annette leaped up, and we all burst out laughing. She glowered at Penny.

"Some friend you turned out to be!"

"We're all friends, and we're all getting up," Penny told her.

Annette almost flopped back down, but Jean, who was trying to pull on her shoes, suddenly let out a yelp. Everybody looked at her.

"What is it?" Scruggs asked.

"My feet!"

He strode around the fire to her and bent down.

"Let me see it," Annette said. But Jean had pushed her foot to Scruggs. He pulled off the two layers of socks and frowned. "Pretty swollen, isn't it?" he asked. "And it's raw. Let's see the other one."

We came up and looked. The other was no better.

"She can't wear her shoes, and that's a fact," Penny said.

"I can carry her," Scruggs said.

Jean burst out crying.

"Come on, Jean, nobody's blaming you," Penny said. "Anybody can get blisters."

But I felt bad for her. Jean was the youngest, and we were always saying—before this, I mean—that she was too young to go with us. I was sure she felt like nothing but a nuisance.

"I'm sorry," she said. "I wish I had stayed home. I'm sorry."

Scruggs forced a grin. "I think we all wished that we'd all stayed home," he said. He looked at Penny and me. "Why don't you go down to the stream?" he asked. "Time's wasting."

"Come on, Annette," Penny said. Annette looked rebellious at being told what to do, but even Jean told her to go on.

"Scruggs sure thinks he knows everything," Annette muttered as we went down to the stream.

"Scruggs has been looking out for Jean since last summer," Penny told her. "And Jack and I didn't like it at first, but now we don't mind. And Jean can't help the blisters."

"What for?" she asked. "She's so much younger than he is. Can't he make friends his own age?"

"Mrs. Bennett thought it would be good for him, I think," I told her. Mrs. Bennett was Scruggs's foster mother.

"Oh her!"

A long time ago when Annette was bossing Jean around, Mrs. Bennett had helped Jean see that she didn't need to be bossed around by older kids. (She was Jean's Sunday School teacher.) I guess she had taught Jean to say *no* in a quiet but firm way. I'm not sure of all that had happened, because that had been while Scruggs and I had been in the Yukon. But anyway, we'd come back to find an older and slightly bolder Jean on our hands, and then Scruggs had tried to take her under his wing as much as he could.

Actually, I think that Annette thought that Mrs. Bennett was an interfering old lady who didn't like her. And Annette had never liked Scruggs. He'd been the neighborhood bully for a long time, before he'd gone to live with Mrs. Bennett, and a lot of people still didn't really trust him and didn't want their kids hanging around him. I think that Annette's parents were in that group. Annette was always talking about how Scruggs was faking everyone, but I think she was just parroting what she'd heard some grown-ups say.

We went and got our drink from the cold stream.

"Whew!" Penny exclaimed.

We finished drinking and stood up.

"Maybe we ought to wait a few minutes," Penny said. "If they're talking, I mean."

"You two would jump over the moon if Scruggs asked you to," Annette said.

"Or pitch you over it," I added.

"Jack!" Penny exclaimed.

"I don't know why you tag along after a kid who can't make friends his own age," Annette added.

"That's no worse than younger kids who are always playing up to older kids," I told her. "Like you do to Penny!"

"Would you guys knock it off?" Penny asked. "We all just became friends, okay? And nobody's the same age as anybody else."

No Friend of Mine

"Annette's no friend of mine!" I exclaimed. "And I sure wish she'd stayed home! Starving in the woods ain't nothing compared with having to drag her along!"

Annette swallowed, and I realized—with some shock—that I'd really hurt her feelings. But all she said was, "You just wait, Jack; you think you're so smart! We've been going wrong the whole time. We should have stayed at the van!"

"Come on, you guys!" Scruggs yelled from up at the camp. "We're thirsty!"

Without another word, we all started back up to the camp.

Chapter Ten

Hunger

After everybody had gotten water from the stream, we repacked the knapsack and got our gear together. The morning was chilly but clear. At least we didn't have to worry about snow. Not yet, anyway.

Everybody wanted breakfast. Hunger was no joke anymore. But Scruggs shook his head. "We're on our last rations as it is," he said. "Let's at least try to last it out until tonight."

Penny was on his side about it. Now that plain and uninterrupted starvation was looking us in the face, she was willing to hold it off at least for a few hours longer.

"But it won't make any difference," Annette said. "It's only going to amount to a few hours in the end."

"A few hours might make a difference," Scruggs told her. "Especially a few hours of daylight. We'll eat lunch between eleven and noon if you want. But let's try to go forward now and just tighten our belts."

For once I was with Annette. I couldn't see what difference it made, and I was getting so hungry that I felt dizzy. But then, if it came to standing and arguing on an empty stomach or walking on one, I'd rather walk. So I was the one who simply said, "Come on, let's go."

But then there was some argument on whether or not to follow the trail or follow the stream. We hadn't run out of water yet, but there was no knowing.

"If we run out of food I don't much care if we have to scramble for water or not," Scruggs said. "I think we should follow the trail all day in hopes of finding help. A trail will take us somewhere faster than a stream will."

Annette and Penny wanted to follow the stream, but I voted with Scruggs, and so did Jean, even though she couldn't walk.

So at last we moved on, with me carrying the pack and Scruggs taking Jean. He still had the guide stick or axe handle in his belt, hung like a sword.

We had to rest more often that morning, because we were all footsore. Annette didn't say much at all. She seemed to be sulking.

A steady breeze had picked up, even though the sky stayed clear. We did find plenty of water on our way. It was hard to get our hands wet to drink it, because the air was so chilly and none of us had gloves or mittens.

At last Penny said what I'd been thinking. "I don't think it's warming up today."

Scruggs glanced at her. He had a fine film of sweat on his face from carrying Jean on his back.

"I think she's right," I added.

"Big deal," Annette said. "Come on."

Scruggs shrugged Jean higher onto his back. "There's nothing we can do about it," he said. He looked both tired and desperate, but there was a kind of light in his eyes—a certain look that I'd seen before when things had been tough. He knew what it meant: if the temperature didn't go up at all during the day, then it was sure to drop lower that night. We might freeze. But Scruggs was the only person I knew who could be both scared and brave at the same time. He wasn't going to let the cold break him down into tears. We were going to keep walking. We wouldn't give up until every single hope was past us.

There was only cheese and candy for lunch. "Only cheese for dinner," Scruggs added. "And that will be the last of it, too."

After an hour's rest, we walked on again. I took Jean for a little while. It's not impossible to carry someone piggyback, even if she is only a few inches shorter than you. But I couldn't go for long with her.

Scruggs took her again, and we marched on.

"Look," Penny said, and pointed to a blue stone path that ran off the trail and back up the mountain. We'd all been toiling along with our heads down. I think we'd have gone right by without ever seeing the stone trail, if Penny hadn't kept her head up.

We all stopped. The trail wound up around a bend of trees.

"Which road now?" Scruggs asked. "Should we vote on it?"

"I don't think it's a trail," Penny said. "It's a driveway. Why should trucks come all the way up here to pave a trail with cobblestones? This is a driveway, and the stones are there to get rid of run-off. Come on."

She went on ahead. I wasn't so sure. If a trail was eroding, why not pave it with some cobblestones?

We climbed up after her, but before we even got around the bend, we heard her give a shout of triumph. "A house!" she exclaimed. "There's a house here!"

"We're safe!" Annette exclaimed, rushing past me. I gave Scruggs a hand as he toiled up the steep slope with Jean on his back.

"The Lord really did hear our prayers!" Jean exclaimed. "It was His adventure after all!" She squeezed her arms around Scruggs's neck from behind. "And you acted just like a knight. Wait till we tell Mrs. Bennett!"

He only looked up with tears in his eyes, whether from Jean's honest praise or because she'd hit his Adam's apple with that hug, I couldn't tell.

Chapter Eleven

Exploring

It was a little alarming to find a house out in the middle of nowhere, but as we got closer to it, we saw that there was nobody there. In fact, the place had been locked up.

"It must be someone's summer place," Penny guessed.

"Or a hunting lodge," I told her. "For some serious hunters."

There were heavy shutters on the windows.

"We're going to have to break in," Scruggs said at last.

"Well, you ought to be good at that," Annette told him.

"What if we get arrested?" Jean asked.

"I think that the police—and the owners—will understand, Jean," Penny told her.

"They must have a phone inside," Annette said. "We can call for help."

"Don't be too sure," Scruggs said. "There may not be any lines run out into this wilderness. And if there are, the line to this place might be turned off."

"He's right," I said. "I sure don't see any signs of a telephone line."

We inspected the outside of the place. It was built in the style of a log cabin, though you could see that the wood covering was a facade, and it looked like a split level, with the lower portion underground.

"I think it's a hunting lodge," Scruggs guessed.

He took out his axe handle and rammed one of the shutters with it. The shutter didn't break, but it gave. He quickly slid the handle into the crack between the two shutters and used it like a lever.

Neither the shutters nor the latches were very stout. It looked as if they had been put up more to protect the glass than to keep out intruders.

At last the shutters popped open.

"I think there's a catch on the window, too," Scruggs said, squinting up at it.

"Let me get on your shoulders to look," I told him.

He was weary, but he didn't argue. I scrambled up onto his shoulders and took a look. "Yup," I said. "There's a catch, but I don't think it'll take much to force it. Use the stick again."

He let me down. We set the handle up against the wood frame of the window and pushed. Annette stayed over by Jean, who was sitting on a stump and watching. Penny gave us a hand.

It took several tries, but at last, as we rocked back and forth between thrusts, we heard a sharp crack and the window lock separated. The window was forced up half an inch or so.

"Whew!" Scruggs exclaimed. "Come on." We pushed the window up.

I climbed up on Scruggs's shoulders first and went through the window. The kitchen door was almost right across from me, and even though it had a bolt on it, the bolt opened on the inside without needing a key. I went back to the window.

"Come around front," I told them. "I'll let you in through the kitchen door."

A dusty chill had settled on the house. There was a refrigerator and oven in the kitchen, but in the absolute silence I could tell that the electricity had been shut off. Still, the place had a fireplace, and there had to be pots and pans around, and perhaps canned food. To me it was as good as a mansion right then.

The others came in. We explored quickly. The downstairs was below ground level. There was a laundry room and two rooms full of bunk beds down there. The ground level had the kitchen and dining room, both paneled in wood and with wood furniture. A short flight of about five steps brought us up to the living room, dark because of the shutters over the big picture window. But there was a huge fireplace.

We had climbed in through the dining room. Scruggs and I went to close the shutters if we could and shut the window. Penny and Annette went into the kitchen to rummage around. We joined them.

"The power's off!" Annette exclaimed in disgust. But Penny had found the pantry. It was dark inside, even with the pantry door open. She glanced out at me.

"I can hardly see, but I think there's canned baked beans in here—stacks of 'em."

Scruggs went into the dining room and came back with a kerosene lamp. He lit it and replaced the chimney. We all went into the pantry.

The fluttering light cast waving shadows over everything. Penny let out a small moan of delight. There were baked beans, Vienna sausages, cans of soup, and huge stacks of sealed plastic containers labeled "Flour," "Sugar," "Baking soda," and "Eggs."

I myself had never been too keen on powdered eggs, but at that moment I thought I could learn to like them.

"We'll leave the lamp with you," Scruggs told them. "Get dinner, okay? Jack and I will see what else we can find."

As I'd guessed, there was no phone out anywhere, but Scruggs and I went down into the lower rooms and rooted through the closets.

"There's lots of stuff here we can use along the way," Scruggs said as he carried various camp equipment out for us to look at in the dim room.

I looked at him. "Use along the way?" I asked.

"Sure."

"You talk as though we're going to be leaving again."

He seemed startled. "We are."

"What? Why?"

"Jack," Scruggs said, "we've got to get out of here before we get a real snow or we'll be trapped for the whole winter. The food won't last more than a few weeks. What if nobody comes?"

"It would be like killing ourselves to risk going through the woods again," I told him.

He shook his head. "Somewhere in this place there will be maps or something to tell us where we are. But if we're within twenty miles of any place with a telephone, we've got to try to get there before a deep snow ends our chances of getting out of here at all."

I shook my head. "No," I said. "This is something we're going to have to vote on. I can't stand the thought of going out there, or of sending Jean out there again."

We looked at each other in the darkening room. "I guess we'll all have to vote on it," Scruggs said.

Chapter Twelve

Fireside Talk

Scruggs didn't say anything else about leaving when we came back upstairs. Without another word to me, he took another kerosene lamp and went back downstairs, leaving me in the living room with Jean.

There was a woodpile outside, and wood to be brought in, so I set to work doing that.

When I was finishing that, Scruggs came up with another knapsack he'd found downstairs. He had packed it full of various tools and utensils for camping.

The cold from outside was penetrating through the walls. We got the fire going.

"I guess we'll all have to sleep by the fire again," Scruggs said.

There had been a cast-iron skillet in the kitchen, and the girls brought it in, filled with canned baked beans. After the fire had burned for a while, Penny used some of the fireplace tools to rake and scrape out some coals toward the stone ledge, and she carefully set the skillet on them. It was too hot to try to cook right at the fire itself.

Scruggs took one of the lamps and went into the kitchen. He also took his knapsack.

"Scruggs wants to move on from here," I told Penny in a low voice.

"I was wondering about that," she whispered back.

"What do you think?"

"I don't know."

She was quiet for a few seconds while she stirred the beans with a long-handled spoon. Then she glanced over at Jean, who was dozing on the couch with her feet propped way up.

"There's no water here for one thing," she whispered to me. "It's been shut off. We found some cans of soft drinks in the pantry, but they wouldn't last us forever."

"Well, a stream can't be too far away," I told her.

"Annette went out to find one," she said.

"She did?"

"Sure. Annette's not too bad," she told me. "You just have to know how to take her."

"Penny, she hates Scruggs, and she's been causing him trouble since this whole thing started."

"I feel sorry for Annette," she told me.

"Why?"

She didn't answer me. Instead, she shrugged and then added, "I don't know whether to move on or stay. When it's lighter outside we can ransack this place for a map. That would be one step in the right direction."

I nodded. "Then there's no point in arguing about it tonight," I said.

"None," she agreed. "Let's eat as much as we can and rest, and then we can decide what to do. But if it were to snow," she added, "we'd be trapped here until spring, and if there aren't any hunting rifles here, we'll certainly starve. There isn't that much food in the pantry."

"Whoever owns this place would probably come up between now and spring," I told her.

"We can't be sure of that."

Just then Annette came back in, and so did Scruggs. I could tell from the way he carried the knapsack that he'd filled it. He set it down against the wall and said, "We'd better bring blankets up from downstairs. Come on, Jack."

"Okay." I scrambled after him.

"No water," I heard Annette saying to Penny. "Not that I found, anyway. But just think, by this time tomorrow night, we'll be safe somewhere."

Scruggs stopped on the steps and almost said something, but then he thought better of it and went downstairs.

We brought up the blankets. By that time Jean was up, hobbling around on her bare feet.

"How are they?" Scruggs asked.

"The blisters aren't too bad without the shoes on," she said.

We had the last of the cheese with the baked beans, and it was a pretty merry meal. Nobody really wanted to talk about future plans. It was enough just to sit and eat and feel warm and safe. The soft drinks were warm, but nobody minded. I'd never liked Vienna sausages, but when Penny passed them around for dessert, I had some.

The fire in the fireplace was only partly able to drive out the cold. We threw blankets around ourselves like Indians—or Vikings, Scruggs insisted—and sat with our backs against the furniture, facing the fire.

"Must be going down to twenty tonight," he remarked. "I'm glad we're inside."

"I guess the Lord answered our prayers," Penny added.

"Speaking of that, let's have a song," Scruggs suggested.

I hadn't really felt like singing or praying, but I obediently straightened up. We sang a few hymns, and I guess it was that more than anything that made us all quiet. We started to think about home. Nobody said anything about praying just yet.

"I guess our folks know we're missing by now," Scruggs said at last.

"I hadn't even thought of that," I told him. "They must be worried about us."

"I guess your mom and dad will have my mother come over, don't you think?" Scruggs asked.

"Sure," Penny said. "They wouldn't let her stay by herself and worry over you."

"Of course," he added, "Mother doesn't worry about much, but I hate to think of her by herself."

"To them we're just missing," Jean added after a moment. "They don't even know that we're in the woods—pretty safe, now."

Penny nodded, and I realized what Jean was hinting at. They didn't even know that we were alive. We were just missing to them. They would be wondering—were we dead, or alive, or in pain, or scared?

"Of course," Scruggs added after a long and silent pause, "they'll pray for us. If God could get us to a house before the temperature dropped, He could send them some sign or some hope that we're all right. Don't you think?"

"If they really cared, maybe," Annette said suddenly. We all glanced at her. She had been mighty quiet during our conversation. She didn't say anything else, and she kept her head down.

"Of course they care," Jean said. There were kids at church whose folks never came, of course, and there were even kids there who had come from homes like Scruggs had once belonged to, where maybe the parents didn't care all that much. But all of our parents were pretty good parents. I guess I didn't like Annette's folks because they didn't like Scruggs, but they'd always been nice to Annette. I felt annoyed with her.

"Well, anyway," Penny said, "it's time to pray, and we can pray for our parents. Right now they might be a lot more miserable than we are."

Chapter Thirteen
A Viking Story

Even though we were praying for just about the same things—safety and rescue and being returned to our parents, as well as giving thanks for the food—we really all prayed a little bit differently, too. Jean was normally just as shy as anyone about having people listen to what she prayed, but that night as we sat in the circle with our eyes shut and taking our turns, she said, "Lord, we know that You brought us safely to the lodge, and You've answered all our prayers so far. So we know that You can answer the same prayers from our folks. Make them understand that we're safe and we've found food. You've given us peace; please give them peace too."

She was the last one to pray, and in that moment of silence when she'd finished, I admired her because she'd asked for something good. And at the same time, I felt like the Lord was close by. Maybe the others felt that way too.

We were quiet again after our prayers, but after a while we started to talk about other things. My camera strap had worn a raw place on my neck. I took it off.

"I wonder if there's first-aid cream in this place?" I asked.

Jean wiggled her toes. "I hadn't thought about that," she said.

But now that night was on, I didn't really feel like exploring through the house in search of anything.

"It must be time for a Viking story," Scruggs said. "Isn't that what they did at night—tell the stories of their old heroes?"

I nodded. "That's right. The bards sang the stories."

"Well, I can't say I'm willing to sing for all of you," he told us with a laugh.

"I think we ought to name your sword," Penny said. "Famous Vikings always had famous swords that were named and treated like mascots."

"Sure, like King Arthur's sword, Excalibur," I said.

"And Caudimordax, the sword of Giles of Ham," Jean said.

Scruggs laughed. "I can't think of any great and noble names in English, and I don't know any Viking languages."

"Let's make one up," Penny said. "Something with an X sound in it, like the other two have."

"How about Lumberjax?" I asked. "Since we found it in a lumber camp."

"Suits me!" Scruggs exclaimed. "Lumberjax!"

"Okay, sword bearer!" Penny ordered. "Up and tell us a story, or you forfeit Lumberjax!"

"That's right!" I agreed. "Any Viking worth his cheese has to cough up a noble story for his peers."

"Half a sec'," Scruggs said as he fastened his blanket over his right shoulder. Then he leaped to his feet and drew the axe handle. "All hail and well met, friends," he announced. "I am Leif, the first son to that noble shield woman who adopted me. I've come to tell you a story about the mysterious washing machine."

"Say on!" Jean called.

He bowed to her. A very slight stubble had sprouted on Scruggs's chin, and he did look a little bit like a Viking teenager.

"Not so long ago in one of the fair hamlets of this unknown country, there sat a washing machine. Yet 'twas no ordinary machine, for it had come from certain government agents unfriendly to this place and to our freedoms. They had set it among other innocent machines, and it had been sold, as custom dictated, to a small family with a little boy. A little boy named Irving."

"Irving?" Jean asked.

"Aye, poor lad, and if that wasn't bad enough, Irving was one of those naughty boys who was always opening up the washing machine to watch the clothes swirl around, a habit—I fear, that indicated other grave flaws in his character. One day, as things fell out, Irving—clean contrary to obedience—opened up the washing machine to watch the agitator run. Of course the machine stopped, but he quickly pushed the black button that he knew so well would make it keep on spinning. And as it spun 'round and 'round, and 'round and 'round, and 'round and 'round, little Irving began to forget who he was and what he was until a voice, carried by radio transmitter cleverly attached to the agitator, said, 'Irving, we order you to go and steal Lumberjax, that famed and deadly sword, from its owner Leif, and from his noble band of Viking friends: Eric, Ooné, Berwyn, and Grendel!' " Scruggs bowed and sat down.

"Is that all?" Penny asked.

"I can't think of everything," Scruggs told her. "The noble band has to come up with the ending."

"Hmm," Penny said. "Since we're the noble band, there's only one answer."

"What's that?" Jean asked.

"As Irving approached us, the noble band struck."

"Struck what?" I asked her.

"What else can a noble band strike? We struck up a tune," she told me. "And the music was so bad that it cleared Irving's head, just like a slap would do. Then we leaped on him and made him promise not to open the washing machine any more to watch the clothes spin. For many a fine lad has been brought to a grim end by such things. And then we took Lumberjax and smote the washing machine and destroyed its transmitter."

Annette hadn't been saying much all this time, but now she said, "You call that a story? How about this? Irving smote Leif with Lumberjax hard enough to make his brains ring. But since Leif didn't have any, all Irving got was a sore hand, and Lumberjax was smashed to pieces."

"Annette!" Jean exclaimed.

Penny and I looked at her. Even I was surprised.

"After all that Scruggs has done—" Penny began.

"Oh, hold off, Penny," Scruggs said. "Just never mind. All she wants is a reaction."

I felt pretty sore inside. Just when it had seemed like Annette was somehow becoming one of us, too! She just couldn't clamp down on how much she hated Scruggs, but what had brought it out like that? Ever since we'd been talking about home she'd been sulking like a two-year-old.

"It's getting close to ten," Scruggs said. "We've got a lot to do tomorrow, and a lot of choices to make. What about tonight? Do we keep a watch?"

I shook my head. Annette didn't answer.

"I'll go along with whatever you decide, Scruggs," Jean told him. She meant it sincerely, but I saw Annette shoot her a poisonous glare.

"I don't think we need it," Penny said.

"Besides," I added with a laugh, "we needed it last night and the watch fell asleep, but nothing happened."

Scruggs shook his head and repeated the term that Penny had coined. "Viking dropouts."

"I'll say," Annette muttered in a low voice. Scruggs ignored her, but it was with an effort.

"Well," he said. "Let the girls get nearer to the fire, and Jack and I will at least sleep nearer the doors. That way if anything happens, we can get out first."

All of us except Annette laughed at that, and we bedded down.

We dropped off to sleep pretty quickly, and I only woke up once to feel the cold driving in through the stairway door. I saw Scruggs get up and put a lot more wood on the fire. The flames roared up, and in the new wave of warmth, I went back to sleep.

Chapter Fourteen
The Map

The sky wasn't clear the next morning when we woke up, but it wasn't threatening.

"Not yet, anyway," Scruggs said.

"A few clouds don't mean snow," Penny told him. "Snow or not, we couldn't leave today. Jean's feet are still bad, and we ought to restock carefully. Not to mention looking for a map."

"I've got a whole pack full of gear ready to go," he told her. "But I agree we have to find a map if we can. And if we can find water, we ought to tote some up here."

"My feet aren't too bad," Jean spoke up. "I think I could get around a little." She grimaced when she put her shoes on, but she did stand up in them and walk around.

We ate canned food for breakfast. It was later than we'd planned, because we'd overslept. Jean and Annette went out to find water if they could, taking a couple of buckets with them as well as a canteen that Scruggs had found.

We went through the house. Scruggs brought up an old newspaper that he'd found. The front page on it showed that it had come from Millinoket, Maine. That encouraged us, just knowing where we were, until Penny pointed out that the newspaper might have been brought up by an out-of-town hunter who had visited the lodge.

At last we made two really valuable discoveries: a map and a pair of field glasses. The map was a terrain map, the kind that you can order through sporting goods stores. It had three different X's marked on it.

"Great," Scruggs said. "Which one is us?"

"Well, they're all close together," Penny said. "If each X stands for a house, we can fan out from here and see if the other houses have people in them."

"But they might not all be houses," I said. "They might be anything at all."

"Wait a second," Penny added. "Look at all those lines labeled as roads. This doesn't even look like a map of this area. We haven't seen any roads yet."

Scruggs shook his head. "No, on these maps all the trails are called roads." He put his finger down on a big square. "Look, this whole section is marked *Great Northern.*"

"So?" we both asked.

"Great Northern is the name of a paper company up here," he told us. "I saw ads for them in the magazines on the plane. That huge deforested place that we saw could be this place on the map. Pulp and paper companies use lumberjacks to get their raw materials."

"That sounds likely," Penny said. "But that patch on the map takes up acres and acres. Where did we come in?"

"Well, we were going south and following a trail all the way down from the perimeter of the logging area." He frowned and studied the map. One squiggly line

snaked up parallel to the Great Northern square and then snaked away.

I placed my finger on it. "I think that's us," I said. "This trail comes down around the deforested area, touches a stream, and then comes up to this X on the map right here. Just like the trail we followed, and so this X must be us."

"I think you're right," Scruggs said. "And look, according to this, if we follow this trail long enough, we come out to Highway 5, and that stops by a town called Andover. Looks to me like it's about fifteen miles from here."

"What about these other X's so close by?" Penny asked.

"Here's a legend on the back of the map," I said as I examined it. "Somebody wrote in with pencil: *Machine shed, one 110 and two 220s. Garage, 110 only.*"

Penny frowned. "What's that mean?"

"I think it answers our questions," Scruggs said. "Those other two X's are outlying buildings to this place. Somebody wrote down the voltage listings for them to remember what machines and appliances to put where."

Even by daylight, it was dim in the main room because we'd left the shutters up and closed. We had one of the lamps lit. Scruggs set the map down on the floor where we were sitting.

"Fifteen miles isn't so bad," he said. "We could do it in a day, if we started early. Even if it took two days, we've lasted a night in the woods before."

Penny looked thoughtful. "But it's so hard on Jean—and Annette, even though she's too proud to say anything." She shrugged. "And the map may not be accurate enough. Even though it has a key, we'd need a ruler and string to know the real distance. What if it's closer to twenty or twenty-five miles?"

"One thing is for sure," Scruggs said. "If we wait for snow, we'll never get there. We'll never get anywhere. We'll die right here."

"Don't be so dramatic," she told him.

"I'm telling you the truth," he said.

At last I agreed with Scruggs. "He's right. Nobody will know to check here for us. If it snows, we'll be stuck for the whole winter. And there's no guns or anything here. We couldn't hunt or anything."

"And," Scruggs added, "there's no guarantee that whoever dumped us off isn't going to decide to come back to do something worse to us. He's the only one who has any idea of where we are."

Just then the kitchen door slammed, and we all jumped. Scruggs put his hand on Lumberjax, in case. But it was only Annette and Jean. Jean was limping again, but I hardly noticed that.

"We found water, but we think there's someone out there," Annette said.

All three of us sat up, tense. "Maybe it was a bear or deer or a moose," Jean added. "But we heard something all right. It was forcing its way through the underbrush, and then it stopped when it was near us. We waited and waited, and finally we went to look, but we couldn't find anything. We came right back here."

"You didn't see any tracks?" Scruggs asked.

They shook their heads.

"Could have just been a deer," Penny said.

"Maybe we ought to check," Scruggs began, starting to stand. We all grabbed him and pulled him down.

"Don't be crazy!" Penny exclaimed. "What if it is a bear? Or someone else?"

After a moment he nodded. "Let's get this place battened down, then. Jack, there was a hammer and some nails downstairs. Let's go nail shut that window that we forced open. If anything happens and we have to get out of here, the packs have to go with us," he said to all of us. "Our lives hang on them."

Everyone, even Annette, nodded. "Come on Jack," he said.

Chapter Fifteen
Figuring Out the Angles

None of us paid much attention to Jean's feet for a while. Penny and Annette went to make lunch, and they yelled for me to come down and help them open some cans. Scruggs went on a patrol of the inside of the house, trying to ensure that everything was as tight as it could be.

But when I got back up to the living room, Jean had her feet propped up again on the couch, and her socks were off. She looked pretty unhappy, and I saw from the redness of her feet that her short walk and brief run through the trees had irritated all the raw skin under the blisters. It was mostly the tops of her toes and the balls of her feet that were raw, although she did have a cut on the back of her left heel, too.

"You must have done too much too soon," I told her.

She didn't answer me, and I could see that she was really mad at herself and her feet.

"Maybe I was too young to come," she said.

"Now who said so?" I asked her. I wanted to take her mind off her problems, so I picked up the newspaper that Scruggs had found and opened it. "Maybe there's some comics in here," I told her. "We could read them."

"I don't much feel like comics," she told me.

But I started to read some of the headlines to her, and then some of the better articles, and at last she got interested. Annette and Penny came in to do the cooking. At last Scruggs came back in, but he left the doorway to the downstairs kitchen open so that he could hear the sounds of the house better.

By that time Jean had one section of the paper, and I had another one.

"Hey look, Jack," she said. "Doesn't this look like the man who got into your picture?" she asked.

"Hmm?" I asked. I glanced at him. "No, Jean, I never saw that guy before."

"Well, that's just like him," she told me. "The man who was so surprised when you took his picture."

Scruggs came over and looked. "Yeah, that was one of the men on the plane with us," he said. "Got on at Boston."

Of course, then Penny and Annette had to come and look. "I think he does look like one of the men on the plane," Annette agreed. "He sat in the smoking section and just smoked one cigarette after another." She wrinkled her nose.

Scruggs pulled a frown. "Phew! How could anybody have missed a guy like that?"

For once Annette was pretty open. "I remember thinking that if he was smoking so hard because flying made him nervous, the smoking would kill him a lot more surely than flying would."

Penny shook her head. "I hardly noticed him. I can't decide whether he looks familiar to me or not. What's it say? Hmf! No wonder he's nervous! He's being investigated for getting kickbacks."

"What's a kickback?" Jean asked.

"It means that this guy has a job with the government," Scruggs told her. "And he gets government organizations to hire certain companies to do necessary work. But then those companies pay him a certain percentage for getting them the big contracts. That's called a kickback."

"Even if the companies do a good job for the government?" she asked.

He nodded. "The guy is allowed to suggest certain companies to do jobs, but he's not supposed to get a private gain from doing it. That's a kickback."

"Says here his name is Hunter Robyns," Jean said. "And he claims that he's innocent. Wow! This article says that federal investigators have linked him with possible fraud and laundering operations."

"If he's innocent, he's sure got a lot of troubles right now," Scruggs observed.

"But if he's guilty, he may think that Jack's taken his picture for some reason," Penny added. "Maybe that *is* where our troubles started."

"Thanks!" I exclaimed.

"Really," Jean insisted. "He was alone on the plane, but not at the airport. Maybe that other man was somebody who Hunter Robyns wouldn't want to be photographed with. Like a man from one of those companies that might be giving him the kickbacks!"

"But why ship us out to the middle of nowhere?" I retorted. "Why not just get that crony of his to hold us up at gun point and swipe my camera?"

"Well, sending us out here would have been one way of making sure that none of us ever identify him or his cronies," Scruggs added.

"Oh, come on," Penny said, impatient. "If he'd wanted to keep us quiet, he could have done something a lot more convenient to him and more efficient."

"That's true," I said. "We all noticed how easy it would have been for that fake driver to have just let the van roll backward down the mountain while we were asleep. But he didn't do it."

"Probably because murder would be a much more serious charge than accepting kickbacks," Scruggs added. "But he has gotten us out of the way effectively enough."

"Only for the present," I said.

Penny shook her head. "Maybe we're on to something, but I think we're still missing what it is. If this man in the paper had something to do with us getting stranded out here, I don't think we've figured out all the angles yet."

"The soup's going to burn," Scruggs added, sniffing the air. Penny and Annette hurried back to the fireplace.

"Meanwhile," Scruggs said with a glance at me, "we've *got* to get water. I plan to go out there and get some. And to take a look around."

Penny turned sharply around. "What if you don't come back?" she asked. "What then?"

"I'll come back," was all that he said. He took the canteen that he'd found, as well as a big pot from the kitchen, and left, exiting through the kitchen.

Chapter Sixteen
Annette

Scruggs did come back, just like he'd promised, and he brought water with him.

"Nobody's out there, as far as I could see," he said. "I was pretty quiet and careful and took a look around for tracks, but I didn't see anything."

"If somebody had been out there, he would have seen you as soon as you'd walked out the door," Annette said.

"The kitchen door's pretty sheltered," he told her. "Not like this front door here, that opens right out in front of the driveway." And he pointed at the front door that opened onto an outside porch.

Annette had no argument with that, and so Scruggs continued, "Meanwhile, we'd better leave our names and addresses here so that the owners know what happened when they come back and can contact us to get their stuff back."

"Well, if you think I'm leaving this place to go out there into who-knows-what, you're crazy," Annette told him.

ABANDONED

"Annette," I said, "it would only be another day's walk to a real town with real people who can get us to my Uncle Bill."

"Can it, Jack," Scruggs said, letting his annoyance with Annette show for the first time. "Let's vote on it."

"I say go," I voted.

"Me too," Scruggs said.

We looked at the girls. I expected them to all vote to stay, but Jean said, "Well, I think we ought to go, too. It seems silly to flop right here until we get snowed in when help is only a day away."

We all looked at Penny. The vote was on our side already, but it was only right to listen to her. She was next oldest after Scruggs.

She shook her head. "If that was a bear—or a person—out there, then I think we ought to stay put. And besides, it may or may not be a day's walk to that town. We have no idea what the terrain might be like. I think we ought to stay."

Annette flashed us a look of triumph that drove me wild with anger. "It doesn't matter," I said quickly. "The vote is three to two—to go."

"Well, go then," Annette snapped. "We'll stay."

Penny shook her head. "No, if the vote is to go, I guess I'll go, too. We've only made it so far by sticking together."

Annette gave a flounce of her head and shoulders. "You Derwoods would do anything that he told you to!" she exclaimed again, meaning Scruggs. "Well, I'm staying! And even he can't *make* me go!"

Scruggs's anger finally flashed out. "Stay then!" he exclaimed. "There's nothing I'd like better than to be rid of you. But we're taking all that equipment that I packed. And you can just do with whatever is left!"

"That's just what I thought I'd hear from you, Scruggs Grady!" she retorted. "Since all you know how to do is steal from people and take their things and then leave them stranded. Just like you stole my knapsack at the beginning of this and haven't even let me carry it."

I thought that what Annette said was nonsense. I think that if she'd said it to me I would have just laughed at how ridiculous it was. But boy, did it make Scruggs mad. Annette could see that as well as I could, and so before he could say anything, she pushed the knife in a little further.

"Everybody knows you're nothing but a thief and a vandal. Good for nothing, and you've got everybody at church and at school snowed, but not me! Nothing's going to change you. You were a bum to start with, and you'll always be a bum!"

"That's not true!" Penny exclaimed.

And even Jean sat up and yelled, "That's a lie!"

But that wasn't half of what Scruggs said.

"You're always onto me because I come from such a bad family," he told her. "And because I was so bad. Well, that's none of your business!" She only smirked at him, but he went on. "I know I'm a Christian now, and all that's been forgiven. But let's talk about you, Annette." There was something in the way he said it that wiped the smirk right off her face. I glanced sharply at him.

"Scruggs!" Penny exclaimed, warning him. Penny sounded scared.

"Let's talk about bad families and lousy homes!" he yelled. "Let's talk about them, Annette! What have you got to say? The whole reason you're on this trip is because your own parents are getting a divorce! Why else would Jack's parents have heaved you off on us when they know we can't stand you? They were trying to get you out of the way so they could talk to your folks. But we all know the truth! They're getting a divorce!"

He was panting when he stopped. I was stunned. I knew it was true. I realized that somehow Penny had known all along. That's why she'd been trying so hard to be nice to Annette.

Jean looked just as big-eyed and scared as I did. Our dad is a deacon, and it's true that Annette's parents had been having my folks over on Tuesday nights for a few weeks.

We all looked at Annette. Scruggs didn't really look sorry yet for having spilled her secret, but at least he had stopped. He was looking at her, too.

"That's a lie!" she screamed. "That's a lie, and you're a liar! And—and I hate you! I hate all of you!" Then she ran out into the kitchen.

Penny looked stunned—not like she hadn't known already about what Scruggs had said, but like she couldn't believe it had come out like that.

"Do something!" Scruggs said to her. She nodded and went after Annette.

"Poor Annette!" Jean whispered. Neither one of us disagreed with her.

Chapter Seventeen

Keeping Watch

I kept myself busy with the soup at the fireplace, and Scruggs poured out some of the water into a smaller basin for Jean's feet. He set the metal basin on the hearth, to take some of the chill out of the water.

A little later, Penny and Annette came back, but Annette wouldn't even look at Scruggs, or at any of us for that matter. If she spoke at all, it was to Penny.

Scruggs wouldn't touch the water in the canteen, but we took what water was left and went into the kitchen to wash up the dishes from the day before as well as we could.

I didn't say much to him while we were at work doing that. I think he was starting to be sorry for all that he'd said. But it's hard to know that people really dislike you for the way you were born and raised. I think if I'd been Scruggs, I would have hated Annette all along, and I would have let it show, too.

It slowly dawned on me that my way of looking at things probably wasn't the right way. We were learning in church about forgiving other people and loving your enemies. I'd never been able to do that—not for very long, anyway. Scruggs had held out more than any other kid I'd ever seen. He'd always at least been polite to Annette—as polite as she'd let him be.

Then I thought about Penny. No matter what Annette had said or done on this awful trip, Penny had never said anything back to her. I had thought that Penny was afraid to stick up for Scruggs. But now I realized that Penny was doing more than just "being nice" to Annette. Somehow, Penny had learned to really love Annette. Even though it looked to me like Annette had just been using Penny, hanging around an older kid to look good. A lot of kids do that.

As I thought about it, I realized that both Penny and Scruggs had treated Annette a lot better than I had, but they were the ones with the best reasons to treat her badly, especially Scruggs. Yet he'd really held out, until just now. It had been more than I'd done. I couldn't blame him for his fall. He'd said some terrible things, and he'd really humiliated her. But still, he'd held out for a long time.

"You're awful quiet," he said at last. "Are you mad at me?"

"No!" I exclaimed, sounding so surprised that he didn't argue. We were silent for a minute as he handed me the cold, wet dishes to dry. At last I said, "I guess I feel bad for Annette, but I feel bad for you, too. She couldn't leave off picking at you and contradicting you every chance she got."

"That's no excuse," he mumbled. "Annette was throwing pebbles at me, but I hit her with a battering ram."

"How did you know?" I asked after a little pause. "About her parents, I mean?"

"Oh, I had it pretty well figured out before we even left," he told me. "There's ways to tell. They never seemed that happy to me anyway. And I could tell from Annette herself the last few weeks at church. And Mother was really concerned and tried to talk to Annette a few times—just cheerful talk, not any questions. But Annette avoided her. And your mom and dad were staying pretty tight with them. I just put it all together. And then when your mom said Annette was coming, I was sure."

"And Penny's known, too," I said. "But I think that for some reason my mom just told Penny."

He nodded. It was getting harder to see him in the gloomy kitchen. Night was falling again. "Penny's been trying to watch out for Annette," he said. "That was obvious."

I thought about that. Penny and I had never held out on each other for very long on anything. We'd grown up like best friends. But now suddenly it seemed like Penny was really a lot older than me—more than just one year. It was like somehow she'd gotten into the circle with all the parents and was trying to help them. Meanwhile, I'd been with the kids, nitpicking and fighting.

We finished and went upstairs. Dinner was silent. There was no singing and no storytelling and not even any praying. I remembered that Penny had wanted to keep watch with me earlier. So when Scruggs said we'd leave first thing in the morning, but we needed a watch tonight, I said, "Penny and I can watch first."

"I'll watch second," he said.

"Me too," Jean offered.

Annette said nothing. I think we all felt really bad that we hadn't included her. But we were all scared to ask her to do anything to help for fear of what else she might say.

Scruggs went down for a last patrol of the house. Then he carefully inspected the pack and secured it. He made sure that the knapsack was as packed as it could be, though we were all wearing the spare shirts and most of the socks. I'd put my camera into the knapsack because it hurt too much to wear it where it had rubbed my neck raw.

Scruggs put his blanket across the front door and lay down there. Annette and Jean went to the fire and bedded down. Penny and I, sitting wrapped in our blankets, sat with our backs against the couch and watched the fire in silence until everybody had at last dropped off to sleep.

You'd think that with a whole day of rest and a big argument in the late afternoon, nobody would sleep much. But everybody seemed even more sleepy than we'd been the night before, as though at last all of our walking and waking had caught up with us.

After a while, I whispered to Penny, "I'm sorry I was so rotten to Annette."

"I know, but it's not up to me to forgive you," she whispered back.

"But she was mean to me, too," I argued.

"I know," she said, and she didn't add anything else. The silence added it for her. I should apologize to Annette anyway. I knew I was supposed to. I just didn't think I could.

We didn't talk much after that, and I felt sleepier and sleepier. The last time I glanced at my watch, it was only ten. The fire was going to coals, and I knew

I should add more wood, but I was so sleepy it was hard to move.

I woke up when the fire flamed up. Scruggs was putting more wood on. Penny was arranging her blanket by the fire. It was one o'clock. He grinned at me. "Go back to sleep, Viking dropout," he said. "Jean and I will take it from here."

I nodded and stretched out on the floor. But I didn't fall back to sleep at first. I watched Scruggs take the basin of water from the fire again and bring it to Jean to put her feet into. She'd been bathing her feet in it off and on since afternoon, just reusing and reheating the same water.

"I guess I'm not much of a Viking," she whispered to Scruggs. He smiled up at her.

"I guess," he added in a whisper, "that I'm not much of one either."

"You haven't been afraid of anything!" she exclaimed.

"I was afraid on the plane," he told her. "I was so scared, I was sick. Don't you remember?"

"I remember that you were sick," she told him.

He nodded. "Well, it was 'cause I was scared. I hate flying."

I said before that Scruggs was a nice kid, but I was surprised to see how good he was with Jean. After she had finished soaking her feet, he used one of the spare shirts to dry them for her; then he carefully fitted his last clean pair of socks over her feet.

"There," he whispered. "A few more days, and they'll be good as new."

I was going to roll over to go to sleep then, but when I turned my head back to the fire, the last thing I saw was Annette, awake, also watching them. She looked sorrier and lonelier than I'd ever seen her look before. That was all it took. I realized that Annette was going through something that I couldn't even picture. And I'd been pretty rotten to her all along. I felt like God had showed me that Himself. Annette wasn't the only person He was working on. I'd been just as stuck-up, but in a different way.

"I'm sorry," I told the Lord. "I promise that I'll apologize to her."

Chapter Eighteen
In Hiding

I fell asleep again, but it must not have been long before something roused me out of my sleep.

Even in my dream I heard a hammering sound that I couldn't figure out, and then as I opened my eyes, I saw the glare of the fireplace and felt myself being dragged a few feet. Scruggs was yelling, "Get up! Get up! They're here! Get up!"

I flailed my arms around crazily until I realized that it was Scruggs himself who had dragged me to wake me up. I jumped to my feet. It was odd that my head was dazed but my body went right on doing what it should have. I stumbled into my shoes.

Penny and Annette were on their feet, pulling on their shoes and gathering up the blankets. Their hands shook as they worked. The hammering sound rang through the whole house. Even Jean had pushed her feet into her shoes, though it must have hurt her.

Downstairs, a window broke. We were all screaming and yelling. There was no doubt now. Somebody had come after us.

ABANDONED

"Don't leave the blankets!" Scruggs yelled. Annette and Penny scooped up a few of them and threw open the great front door.

"Go! Go!" Scruggs yelled. Jean got as far as the door, but I could see that even her fear couldn't overcome her pain. I don't really know how I did it, but somehow in the next second I found her across my shoulders in a fireman's carry. I'd carried her that way once or twice as a joke, but it was no joke now. She had the smaller knapsack in her hand, and we all burst out the doorway together into a night that—at first exposure—seemed bitterly cold.

I stumbled against the porch railing, nearly fell, and found the steps. Ahead of me, Penny and Annette were flying towards the winding drive. The night was clear, with stars. I heard the door slam as Scruggs came out after me with the big pack in his arms.

"Go! Go!" he was still yelling. "Go!" I leaped off the porch and ran.

A gunshot rang out, but we ran on, heedless of it. Nothing seemed more frightening than being captured by whoever was after us.

We stumbled onto the drive and down the slope toward the trail. Scruggs came up behind me.

"Where are the girls?" he cried.

"Up ahead!" I gasped. "I can still hear them."

The trees made the landscape a lot darker, but we got down onto the trail. Scruggs pushed the pack at me and took Jean. "Stay on the trail until you hear me whistle!" he ordered. "Then duck into the woods and don't move. Wait for me to whistle again before you get onto the trail."

ABANDONED

We jogged off. The pack on my back made too much noise for me to hear whether or not anybody was coming after us. Scruggs had put some trail cooking gear into it, and it rattled around.

We stumbled around a bend on the dark trail, and Scruggs's whistle pierced the night. I jumped into the trees and froze. I must have reacted first, because I had time to hear what I took to be Penny and Annette crash into the underbrush up ahead of me and then become silent.

A few seconds later, footsteps came pounding up past me on the trail and passed by. I waited, nearly breathless in the cold woods. It seemed like an eternity went by. I took the time to cautiously pull my socks up higher under my trousers and tie my shoelaces. I buttoned up my overshirt and zipped up my jacket. That helped shut out the night's coldness.

Then I became aware of stealthy footsteps on the trail. I tensed. I had the heavy pack on. If I took it off, whoever was coming would be sure to hear me. But if he already knew where I was, the pack would stop me from fighting or getting away. Just as I was about to throw it off and risk running away, I heard Scruggs's whisper: "Jack!"

"Here!" I whispered back, as loud as I dared.

In another second I saw a clumsy shadow between me and the trees by the trail. He was trying to come silently. At last he got up to me.

"Stay here," he whispered. "Maybe for the rest of the night. They'll think we went the other way and go back. Don't move until you hear my signal."

"Okay," I whispered. "Where's Jean?"

"Back on the other side of the trail. Waiting for me. Where are the girls?"

"Farther ahead, I think," I told him. "This side of the trail."

"Okay. I'll get to them."

He made his way back out as quietly as he could, feeling his way with each foot before taking a step.

He must have gotten to them. A little later I saw him on the trail, skulking along the edge of it before he went back into the trees on his side.

My wristwatch wasn't the glow-in-the-dark kind. Even though I strained to get some glimpse of the hands on it, I couldn't make them out. I tried to figure out what time it was, but all I could do was guess. Scruggs and Jean had come on watch at one, and I had been awake for about thirty minutes and had then fallen pretty deeply asleep. Was it two in the morning? Or later? Five, maybe?

The ground was cold and damp and I didn't want to try crouching on it, either on my seat or on my knees. I managed to get myself propped up against a tree with the pack set into a fork in the trunk. Poised like that, I waited. All around me, the forest was dark, cold, and silent.

I don't know how a person could fall asleep like that. I thought I'd only dozed a little before I heard Scruggs's whistle. Trying to be quiet—but failing—I stumbled out onto the trail on legs that had become numb from the cold and from falling asleep. Though dark, the forest was not as dark as it had been, and I realized that dawn was coming.

"I guess they're safely on their way back up the trail," Scruggs said. "That or looking for us in the woods around the lodge. Let's go."

"Did they run past us again?" I asked.

Penny and Annette had come out together. Penny cocked her head and looked at me. "Didn't you hear them? They ran by about twenty minutes ago."

I shook my head. "No. I guess I fell asleep standing up."

For some reason I felt more exhausted then than I'd felt yet on this misadventure. And I wondered, as we started out, how we would hold out for even fifteen miles with enemies on our trail.

"Absolute silence," Scruggs whispered as we started. "We even have to walk silently. Same plan as before. Hear the whistle, disappear."

We nodded and started out.

Chapter Nineteen
On the Trail

I'd put my camera into the knapsack the night before. I wondered if it was all right after getting jounced and banged around so badly. But there was no time to ask. Penny had contrived to fold the two blankets that we'd rescued into tight little balls, and she'd wrapped a windbreaker around them. She'd used a sweatshirt for lashings to tie it to herself almost like a pack. Annette was carrying the knapsack. Scruggs had Jean, and I had the big pack.

We walked in single file, with Scruggs and Jean bringing up the rear to listen better. Penny stayed up front and kept a watch on the trail. I think that everybody wanted to get out of there more than anything else, and we traveled farther that morning, loaded down as we were, than we'd traveled before.

But the trail began to wind back up a spur of the mountain. I noticed this and hoped at first that it would turn its course, but it didn't.

At last I raised my hand to signal a halt. Scruggs and Jean were the only ones who saw me, so I tugged on Annette's jacket. Penny heard us all stop, and she stopped and joined us, too.

"It's turning the wrong way," I said, still keeping my voice down to a whisper. "The map said southwest, and it's heading back northwest—and back up the mountain," I added.

Scruggs nodded. "It looks like it's just going up to join that lumber area again," he whispered.

"We can't go back," Penny said. "All we can do is go on."

"Even if it does go back up," Annette added in a whisper, "the main trail may branch or fork off and go on south. Just like the trail we came down on. All the lumber trails will join this one, but it ought to go someplace."

We all nodded, and Scruggs signaled for us to keep going on up the trail.

After less than a quarter mile of anxious climbing, we did see the trail branch in two directions—one northwest, and the other southwest. But the one that went southwest was as steep a drop as I'd like to see with a full pack on my back.

"How'd they ever get a truck down that?" I asked.

"Shhh," Scruggs said. "They managed," he whispered. "Mountain trucks are half acrobat. Come on."

We scrambled down the steep trail. Penny and Annette skidded in places, and a couple of times I thought I was going to fall end-over-end, but I didn't. Scruggs came down slowest of all with Jean on his back. She had her eyes shut at first, but then I saw her force them open. I guess she'd figured that if Scruggs had to watch, she ought to watch, too.

"Whew!" he said when at last they'd gotten down safely. He nodded at the trees. "Come on," he said. "Lunch time. No fire."

We ate baked beans right out of the can, which may sound grotesque, but I didn't mind half as much as I would have thought a week earlier. Then we shared water from the canteen. We had to rest. All of us had walked farther and faster than we'd thought possible.

"We've got to have a fire tonight," Penny said at last.

"I hope we're safe in that town tonight," Scruggs told her.

"Well, it's past noon and there's no sign of the highway," she pointed out. He nodded wearily. "We've got to plan for the worst," she told him.

"Nothing could be worse than this," I agreed.

"We have to have a fire at night and that's the end of it," he said. "You can't hide a fire—not if the fire's got to be big and hot. So what's to plan?"

"We could build a reflector," Penny added.

"What's that?" he asked.

"Kind of like a screen. It would at least help to hide it. And it will keep us warmer if the temperature drops so low again."

He nodded. "You'll have to show us." But he looked defeated. I knew what he was thinking. If we didn't make it to that town, we'd have to have a fire. And if we had to have a fire, whoever was chasing us would have an ideal chance to catch us at last.

"That town is our only hope," Annette said softly, putting it into words for all of us. In spite of our troubles, I wondered what was going through her head.

ABANDONED

We were all silent. At last Penny spoke up. "When we started all this, we agreed that we would rather go out and risk it in the woods than be left begging at the van," she began.

We all nodded.

"And we've done pretty well out in the woods," she added. "I mean, we're still in one piece. When we were running out of food, we still played right to the end."

Everybody was looking at her now.

"I think we should go one further," she said.

"What?" Scruggs asked, newly interested.

"We refused to be beggars at the van," she said. "Well, I refuse to be hunted in the woods."

"They have at least one gun," I reminded her.

"Yeah, but that doesn't make me a rabbit," she said. "We're Vikings, remember?"

Everybody nodded, even Annette. "I guess a Viking ought to go down fighting," Scruggs began, but she cut him off.

"Who said anything about going down?" she asked. "I was talking about beating the game. I think we should try to trap those people who are hunting us." She looked around at us. "I think there's two of them," she began.

I nodded. "That's what I'd say."

"Twice now, they could have killed us," Penny added. "But they haven't. I think we could say that they don't want to. But they want something."

"Twice?" Annette asked.

"Once in the van and once last night," I said. "They had a gun and shot a warning shot to try to make us stop."

"So you think we could lure them pretty close," Jean guessed. "But what weapon do we have?"

"Lumberjax," Scruggs said. "There's a hunting knife, but I don't think it would do much good. We don't want to get into any hand-to-hand fighting with these guys."

"Even with Lumberjax," Annette said. "You'd have to get right up behind an armed man to hit him."

"That wouldn't be impossible," Penny said. "Not if we tried to make it as easy as possible to get right up behind him. If we arrange the trap, we should be able to do pretty much whatever we want."

"Well, how?" Annette asked.

"For one, find a place so overgrown and tangled that whoever tries to get close to us has only one route to take. Then we'll know exactly where to spring the trap," she said.

"Well, that shouldn't be too hard," Scruggs said. He looked at Penny with new respect. "You sure know how to put heart into a Viking," he said.

Chapter Twenty
Setting the Trap

"If it's a trap that we want," Scruggs said after a little thought, "I don't think we could do better than this."

Penny looked thoughtful. "Maybe not."

They were right. We were sitting under the shadow of that steep drop. Anybody coming that way would have to pay a lot more attention to his footing than to us—for a few seconds, at least.

"What if they come up the trail the other way?" Annette asked. "They might get out to the highway by some other route and try to sweep their way back to us." She didn't sound like she was finding fault. It was a sensible question.

"I think it's more likely that they split up to search the trails in either direction from the hunting lodge," Scruggs said. "But if we start now, we can make sure that anybody coming up from the highway would still have to sneak around this way where a lookout from above could spot him—if not hit him—and give a whistle."

We did some planning after that. First we moved our gear farther off the trail into as small a clearing as we could find, and we laid the fire, although we didn't light it.

Anybody coming down on us from the trail above would have to use the steep trail that we'd used. He'd make too much noise on that steep slope trying to sneak down on us through the trees. As for the woods on the far side of the camp, we dragged in as much deadwood as we could to tangle it up even more and make it impenetrable. All this was done while Jean kept watch for us at the trailside. One thing she could do was whistle.

Scruggs had twine in the pack, and he used it to make trip lines throughout the trees on the far side of the camp. I used the hunting knife to whack off as many boughs as I could from the evergreen trees. It certainly dulled the knife, but we got a good many, and Penny used them to build a reflector against the cold. We scattered the leftovers around the base of another sturdy but small evergreen, and we made that our hiding place if things went wrong. All of us could crawl under the boughs and hide. It would be a tight fit, but it would work.

We didn't want to give ourselves away and seem too obvious to whoever was stalking us, so we held off lighting the fire and simply watched the trail as the shadows lengthened. Nobody came, but then nobody had come the day before until it had been almost morning, though they'd known where to find us.

As darkness fell, Penny and Annette went to the fire to get it lit. I took Jean there on my back, but then I slipped back through the trees with the two blankets. One I passed up to Scruggs, who was climbing back up the trail to hide in the trees up higher. I hid lower down on the slope. My job was either to help

Scruggs if he needed it or to run and get the others to the hiding place if things went against us.

The reflector that Penny had built was nothing more complicated than a short wall of evergreen boughs lodged between tree trunks. It faced the fire from the woods side and threw back both light and heat. A reflector can either shield your fire or make it more apparent, depending on where you set it.

I could see the fire from where I was hiding with my blanket thrown around my shoulders. Scruggs had fastened his over his shoulder again, and I had imitated him. But even with the blanket, it was cold away from the fire. No falling asleep tonight!

I had agreed with Scruggs about the people chasing us. Very likely they had split up and would be searching in either direction on the trail from the hunting lodge. And they would have to go on foot, knowing that at the first sound of a jeep or truck we'd disappear. So it would take some time for them to reconnoiter and then for at least one of them to catch up with us. I certainly hoped—after all our trouble—that he would catch up with us and sight our fire.

I needn't have worried. A sudden shower of pebbles spilled down the trail as a booted foot slipped on it up above. I tightened my fists. By then the trail was dark. Scruggs was up above me, standing in a clump of trees right on the fringe of the trail, about a quarter of the way down the steep slope. He'd picked a spot where he could step out on a firm place, whack whoever was coming, and get back into the trees again.

But whoever was up above us didn't come down right away. Surely he (or they) could see the gleam of the fire. But it was going to be like the previous night.

He (or they) would wait until the fire had burned low and the camp would be asleep or sleepy.

I waited and waited, my stomach knotted up like a tight ball. I don't know how much time passed with me in that state. Usually when I'm scared, a little time seems like a long time. But when I heard the cautious boot steps start down the trail and saw the low gleam of a flashlight sweep once down the slope, I straightened my knees and found that they'd gone numb. I must have been waiting for him for at least an hour.

Suddenly there was a tremendous whack of wood on bone, and Scruggs yelled, "Come up, Jack! It's just one!" And almost immediately the two of them went rolling down the slope past me, locked together. But the flashlight had dropped on the trail up above, and its light revealed the smooth and shiny barrel of a rifle. I scrambled up and seized both of them, then slithered down the slope. The rocks on the trail dug into my thighs as I went, but I was so excited that I didn't care.

Scruggs and the stranger were wrestling over Lumberjax, of all things. I think that when he got hit, the guy got so dazed that he thought Lumberjax was his gun, and he was trying to get it back from Scruggs. As my flashlight beam hit it, the guy saw what it was and let go without thinking. Scruggs hit him again with it before the guy could correct his mistake, and that crumpled him.

"Are you all right?" I called to Scruggs.

He nodded, but there was blood down one side of his face. He handed Lumberjax to me, and I thrust it into my belt and covered the guy with the gun. Scruggs switched off the flashlight and put it into his pocket.

"Let's get him to the fire," he said.

Chapter Twenty-one

The Interrogation

Our new companion took a few minutes to wake up, and by then Scruggs had dragged him to the fire. I offered the rifle to Scruggs, but Scruggs shook his head. "Just Lumberjax if you please," he said. "I'm really getting to like that sword."

He had gotten a gash on the side of his face while falling down the slope, and his eye looked like it was going to be a fine shiner by morning. Half of his face was a mask of blood, but he wouldn't let any of us help him until we'd settled matters with our prisoner.

In the light of the fire we all recognized him as the man who had driven our van. We'd propped him up with his back against a tree. As he came around, he tried to put his head into his hands, but we'd tied them with some long woolen socks of Scruggs's that we'd cut into strips.

He opened his eyes, squinting in the painful glare of the fire.

"Hail, and well met," Scruggs said with a note of irony in his voice. "Seems like you've stumbled into a Viking camp without permission."

"What are you talking about?" the man asked.

"Who are you?" Scruggs asked.

The man's wits began to return to him. He realized that his hands were tied and that he'd lost his fight with Scruggs and that we were all waiting for him to answer us. He looked at all of us.

"Sam Vierowe," he said.

Scruggs gave a wry smile. "Thanks."

Annette, impatient, exclaimed, "Why did you do all this to us!"

He glanced sharply at her. "Look, girl, you mess with grown-ups and their business, and you pay the consequences!" he exclaimed. "I've never done anything to a kid in my life except clean up bloody knees for them."

"We weren't messing with any grown-ups," Penny said. "We were coming up here to see our Uncle Bill."

Sam Vierowe snorted and looked away.

"She's telling you the truth!" I exclaimed.

"You're the one who took the picture!" he exclaimed back to me. "And if my hands weren't tied, I'd take you over my knee and give it to you till you were black and blue."

My throat tightened and so did my voice. "If you were free and tried to touch me, I'd put a bullet into you," I told him. "You're a fine one to talk about us messing with you. You shouldn't have messed with us. We don't plan on being hunted down in these woods!"

"Not by you or anybody else!" Penny exclaimed.

"So just answer us," Scruggs said. "Tell us what you think we've done."

I think that our coolness, and the fact that we all agreed with each other, shook him a little bit. "You went and took that picture of the man I work for," he said. "He's been good to me and got me a job when no one else would take me on. It's not fair for your folks to keep hounding him like that. And it was pretty low and small for your folks to send you out to the airport to do it. Can't a man have some privacy? It's no crime to talk to someone."

"So," Scruggs said, "that *is* what happened. That really was Hunter Robyns at the airport, and Jack got him and that other guy in his picture." He looked at our prisoner. "But we don't even know the man. Jack just wanted a picture of the airplane."

"Who was that man he was talking to?" Jean asked.

But Vierowe didn't answer that.

"Look," Penny said. "We come from Peabody, Wisconsin. We don't know anything about this man's legal troubles except for what we read in that paper up in the hunting lodge."

"I've never even heard of Peabody, Wisconsin," he said.

"Nobody has," I told him. "But we're not lying."

"It doesn't matter what you think of us or what we think of you," Scruggs said. "It's the camera you want, isn't it?"

After a second, he nodded.

"I get it now," Penny said. "You swiped all of our cases and knapsacks to get the camera, not knowing that it was around Jack's neck. Then when you realized you didn't have the right camera, you had to come back after us."

He didn't answer her.

"That was pretty rotten of you," Scruggs said. "We've been through an awful lot. We might have been killed."

"Oh sure," he said. "It was only thirty miles from any town, and you could have found houses up here—if you'd looked."

"We don't know our way around up here," Scruggs told him.

"Look, if I'd wanted to kill you kids, I could have done that very easily!" he exclaimed.

"Pardon us if we're not grateful," Annette said.

"The question now is what to do with you," Scruggs said. "And by the way, where's your friend?"

But Vierowe wouldn't say. He just looked down. Scruggs took Lumberjax and put the end of it right under Vierowe's jaw and forced his face around.

"Look," Scruggs said. "If we could get out of this with nobody getting killed, I would be very happy. But if your friend tries to sneak up on this camp, he's going to get shot. We can't play games. I'm the oldest one here, and I've got to get all these kids home safely." He lowered Lumberjax. "You decide, mister. I don't want to leave you tied up in these woods alone, but I'm thinking of them first. We didn't ask for this trouble, and we never meant you or Hunter Robyns or anybody else any harm."

When he still didn't answer, Scruggs stood up. "Let's get out of here," he said. "We've got a flashlight now. We'll go as far as we can."

"Wait a second," Vierowe said. "My partner's gone the other way. He'll make back for our jeep at the hunting lodge. We're supposed to rendezvous there at dawn."

"How do we know he's telling the truth?" Annette asked.

"It is a logical story," Scruggs said.

"I don't want to get left in these woods alone," Vierowe said.

"Wasn't that what you planned for us?" Annette asked.

"I didn't tie you up," he reminded her. "Though I could have. Now you said that if I told you the truth, you wouldn't leave me here."

"He's not a crook," I told them. "I don't think he's lying to us."

Scruggs sat back down again. "Check the knots on his hands, Jack. And Jean, wash his face for him and give him a drink. We're staying. I just don't think I could go on tonight anyway."

Chapter Twenty-two
Don't Come Back

Vierowe was probably a little more scared of having fallen into the hands of the kids he'd been chasing than he would have wanted to admit. But he calmed down soon enough.

"What happened to your feet?" he asked Jean as she scooted over to him on her knees.

"They got blisters," she said.

"Thanks to you!" Annette exclaimed.

"Easy does it," Scruggs said.

Vierowe didn't say anything after that, not until Jean had finished wiping the blood off his face, and then he said, "Thank you."

"You're welcome," she told him.

Penny had brought up water earlier, so there was plenty, and Scruggs had included one of those tin coffee-pots that backpackers use.

"Want coffee?" he asked Vierowe.

"I guess," Vierowe said with a nod.

"It'll be black," Scruggs told him. "But it's better than nothing."

"I always drink it black," Vierowe said.

ABANDONED

None of us had eaten since lunch, because we'd been scared to unpack. The beans were all gone, but Scruggs had thrown in a cured bacon and a dry pancake mix. Penny mixed up the pancakes and cooked them, one at a time, on a camp skillet. We had to eat one at a time, but she let Scruggs and me eat first because we'd gotten no sleep. I left the rifle with her. She stayed awake to keep an eye on Vierowe.

It was nearly four o'clock before I got a chance to lie down, but it didn't take me long to fall asleep. Scruggs and I shared one blanket.

We left the other blanket for the girls, but when I woke up at sunrise, I saw that someone had flung the blanket over Vierowe—probably Jean, who was curled up in the other end of the blanket. Vierowe was asleep.

Near the fire, Annette was curled up against Penny, who was still awake, though nodding.

I stood up. "Rise and shine, Penny," I called to her. She smiled a weak smile at me. "I can handle rising, but I won't promise to shine."

Scruggs stirred and woke up with a groan. He'd washed the blood off his face the night before, but he plainly had a shiner on his left eye, and his lip was puffed out.

"Sam Vierowe, it's a good thing for you I don't hold a grudge," he mumbled.

The camp slowly came alive.

"It's about eight miles back to the lodge," Scruggs said as we packed all our gear up. Today we took care to try to divide the weight more between the pack and the knapsack. "No doubt your buddy will be on his way here to find you. If he comes in your jeep or truck or whatever you've got, it won't take him more than about twenty minutes. That doesn't give us much time. But I don't mean to just leave you here."

He untied Vierowe. Vierowe staggered to his feet and winced as the blood got circulating again. Penny kept the gun on him, but he didn't try anything.

"No breakfast?" he asked with a wry smile.

"Sorry, we've been doing without breakfast lately," Scruggs told him. "I don't want to try to march you with us, so I'm going to let you go. But I'm warning you, if you come after us again, we'll have no choice but to shoot."

Vierowe hesitated. "Maybe I was wrong about you," he said. "But if you'd just give me that film, we could call it square, and I would even offer you a ride into Andover."

"We didn't come here to cause trouble for Mr. Robyns," Scruggs said. "But it wouldn't be right to give you that film now, not with what we know. If that picture makes a difference either way, we'll give it to the law."

"You're the most different bunch of kids I've ever seen," Vierowe said. "I wish we could have done all of this differently."

"Go back up the trail," Scruggs told him, "and if you and your friend don't want a gunfight, don't come after us again."

Vierowe gave a brief nod and turned to go up the trail. We watched him climb the slope and then walk along the trail until he was out of sight. Scruggs scrambled up the trail and watched through the field glasses until he was sure that Vierowe wouldn't come back. At long last, when he was satisfied, he scrambled back down to us. Without a word, he took Jean onto his back.

"Do you really think they won't come back?" Penny asked.

"I don't know," Scruggs said. "But we couldn't have watched him and tried to march, too. I think he would have been smart enough to have gotten his gun back somehow."

"If he'd gotten desperate enough, he might have tried to rush us for it," I added. "And—no matter what I said—I'm not sure I could shoot somebody, especially somebody that I've eaten with."

"But surely he knows that we'll turn him in to the authorities," Penny guessed.

Scruggs shook his head. "We might try, but I think that the name Sam Vierowe might just be that man's alias. If Hunter Robyns is as wealthy as he sounds, I'm sure that he'll help Vierowe or whoever he is just fade into the background somewhere else. Come on, let's go."

Scruggs still hung back at the end of the line to listen for sounds of pursuit as we marched, and he used the field glasses to watch up and down the trail, but the morning passed without anything happening.

"Unless they really are following us and are just waiting for night again," Penny guessed.

Scruggs shook his head. "If those guys have any brains, they'll cut around somehow and wait on the highway for us—if they still mean to trap us and get the camera."

"What do we do then?" I asked him.

"Well, we've got to get to the highway," Scruggs told me. "After that, I don't know."

Chapter Twenty-three
The Highway At Last

We found the highway before noon. Scruggs sighted it up ahead of us. The trail simply emptied onto it, and then picked up again on the other side and vanished into the trees.

"Wait," Scruggs called up to me. We all halted, and he signaled us into the trees.

"Here's where it gets scary," he said. "We'll be a lot easier to spot on the highway."

"I just don't think I have the strength to fight my way through the woods," Penny told him.

"But it's more serious now," he reminded her. "They know we have a gun. They may choose to shoot first if they feel desperate enough."

"I don't know," I said. "I don't think Sam Vierowe could kill anybody—least of all kids."

"But what about his partner?" Annette asked. "We don't know about him."

"Maybe we could wait them out," Jean suggested. "Make a secret camp and wait until they give up on catching us."

"We hardly have enough food for one more night," Scruggs told her.

"Can't we follow the same plan?" I asked. "Walk quietly and wait for the whistle?"

"A jeep on the highway could get pretty close pretty fast before we managed to hide ourselves," Scruggs reminded me. "By the time I heard it and whistled, they could have us in their sights."

"But even if that happened," Penny argued, "we've got a gun, and they know we have a gun, and they can't be that anxious to shoot it out with us over a camera."

"Hey," Jean said suddenly.

"What?" Scruggs asked her.

"It's snowing."

We all looked around. She was right. Not many flakes were falling—it hardly looked like more than a flurry. I stepped out onto the trail. The clouds were low and heavy.

"We should have kept a better eye on the weather." Scruggs groaned. "I did notice that it was overcast at dawn, but I've hardly thought about it."

"Nothing would have changed if we had noticed," Annette said. "We'd still be right here, wondering what to do." I glanced at her, surprised. She was right. She even sounded objective. For the first time I thought that maybe Annette was sorry for a lot of things, too.

"You're right," Scruggs said quickly. "But we can't wait around anymore. We've got to risk the highway. Keep close in single file and wait for the whistle."

We set off again, and the only precaution that we took was that we waited on the trail while Scruggs went up to the highway to look around for an ambush. He was gone for about thirty minutes, and it made us anxious to sit and wait for him so long. But at last he came back and waved. All clear.

He took Jean onto his back again, and we started off. That last stretch of miles should have been the most cheerful for us. The road was easy and we knew that there was a town at the end of it. But we were so nervous about being chased and getting cut off at the very end that we hurried along in silence. All of us were limping again. And the snow got heavier. It was not a snowstorm, but it was becoming a good steady snowfall.

It didn't seem to take very long for a film to settle on the road, and Penny's and Annette's feet left clear prints in it. It got slippery, and we had to be careful as we went. I stopped listening for pursuit. I just concentrated on getting one foot ahead of the other. It was like the last four days had made a big wall, and it kept barring the way. I was footsore. I was hungry. I hadn't gotten much sleep.

"Come on, Jack," Scruggs's voice said from behind me. I nodded and tried to hurry. Exhaustion was a fist, and hunger was a fist, and pain was a fist, and they were all punching me back.

"Faster, Jack," Scruggs said again. "Keep up with the girls."

The girls were not carrying that heavy pack.

But just then Penny said, in a clear voice that I'd never heard her use before, "There it is!"

I looked up. The snow was heavier still as it fell, but plain as plain, we could see a town nestled on the road as it sloped down again.

Snow had settled on the bundles that we carried, and it had fallen into Penny's and Annette's hair and on their eyelashes. We all came and stood in a group.

ABANDONED

None of us cried or laughed or yelled or anything. We just stood there for a second, all the Vikings.

"We ought to find the police or a sheriff or something," Scruggs said at last.

"Even the fire department," I added. He gave me a sideways look.

"Come on," he said, and without thinking, led the way.

Chapter Twenty-four
The Famous Picture

There wasn't a hospital in Andover—there wasn't much of anything—and so we were put into a motel cabin, and a doctor came to look at us.

Scruggs and I had one room, and the girls had another. Andover seemed to be entirely made up of motel cabins, so I didn't even know the name of the place where we stayed.

The doctor was a pretty young guy as doctors go—maybe thirty. He had a weather-beaten kind of face, and he was nice. His hair was blond and brown and short. It stuck up straight on his head when he pulled off his cap.

"Guess you boys an't the worse for wear," he told Scruggs and me. "Keep your feet up and take aspirin, and eat as much as you can hold. You'll be right as rain in a few days. Heard you had quite an adventure out in the woods." He admired Scruggs's black eye and put antiseptic on the cut, which made Scruggs yell.

He went to check the girls, and he got slippers for Jean to wear. After that, the state police officer we'd talked to came back to see us, and he brought another officer with him, a lieutenant. We'd already handed the camera over to them. The lieutenant, whose name was Phyler, asked us a lot more questions about what had happened. First he talked to each one of us alone, and then he talked to all of us together.

We knew by that time that we were in a little town in Maine, close to the state line between Maine and New Hampshire. We'd been left off about seventy miles east of Littleton.

"This case will involve the FBI," Lieutenant Phyler told us. "That fellow Vierowe took you across state lines, and so this becomes a federal crime."

"What about Hunter Robyns?" I asked him. "He's the one who told Vierowe to leave us stranded and steal the cameras. I think he's more guilty than Vierowe is."

Lieutenant Phyler smiled and gave a slight shrug. "We have very little evidence against Robyns," he said. "The five of you claim he was involved in this, but even you admit that Vierowe merely told you so. We have no evidence that Vierowe told you the truth."

"But there's the picture," I said.

"That's still only circumstantial evidence, Jack," Scruggs said.

Lieutenant Phyler's grin broadened. "Would you like to see a print of your famous picture?" he asked.

All of us leaned forward to look. He pulled an envelope out of his jacket pocket and drew out the photo. It showed a wall of black with a tiny gray glimmering blob on the right that was, I believe, the nose of the airplane that I'd photographed.

"You ever shoot a picture with a 35-millimeter before?" Lieutenant Phyler asked me.

"No sir," I told him. "But the directions said—"

Everybody was looking at me. We were all sitting at a kind of breakfast table in the small cabin. Penny started to laugh.

She put her head down on the table and laughed really hard.

"Penny," I said.

"All *that!*" she exclaimed. "All that for the nose of a plane!"

"You can't even see the plane, let alone two guys standing alongside it!" Scruggs said, taking the photo and looking at it. I snatched it from him.

"I think I can make out two little silhouettes there," I said.

Jean peered over my shoulder. "I sure can't."

Penny howled with laughter, and then finally brought it under control. "Viking dropouts!" she exclaimed. "We didn't even get a decent focus on the picture that started it all."

We had told the police about playing Vikings (it had embarrassed Scruggs) and Lieutenant Phyler said, "Well, really, I wouldn't call you dropouts. I think you showed a lot of grit out there."

I thought about how much we'd fought and argued the whole way. "Maybe," I said. Annette had her eyes down, too. I guessed that she was blaming herself for a lot of our troubles along the way. Scruggs had been right from the very beginning, and all she had done was argue with him—up until the last night in the lodge, anyway.

"And you did a good job, son," Lieutenant Phyler said to Scruggs. The praise startled Scruggs. He turned red. He glanced at Annette and glanced down.

"Not that good of a job," he said.

The Famous Picture

"We all worked together," Penny said. "And we all made a lot of mistakes."

"Well, this snow's pretty heavy," Lieutenant Phyler told us. "We located your uncle, but I don't know that he'll be able to get through tonight, on account of the snow. Won't be a storm, I don't think, but the roads'll be closed until morning."

"We can wait one more day, I guess," Scruggs said.

"The diner's got food fixed up for you," he told us. "I'll have someone fetch it over."

We thanked him, and he and the other officer left. By that time it was night.

Penny took Jean to their room to get socks for Jean's feet, and Scruggs went back into the room that he and I were sharing. Annette got up to follow Penny.

"I'm sorry, Annette," I said.

She stopped and looked at me. "You don't know anything about it," she told me.

"I know," I said. "But when we were in the woods the last day, I thought I'd like to be friends with you if I could. And when I said I was sorry just now, I meant I was sorry for how I acted all along."

"You never have liked me," she said. "No matter what I've done!"

I realized that she was right. I'd always thought that Annette was just a tattletale and too bossy with littler kids.

"I like you now," I told her.

"Just because you feel sorry for me."

I shook my head, but I didn't know what to say, until at last I told her, "If you'll sit down I'll tell you exactly why I want to be friends with you."

She looked like she had half a mind just to walk away, but then suddenly she plopped down again. So I told her about that last night in the hunting lodge.

"So you do just feel sorry for me," she said when I'd finished.

"I think I feel like I haven't been fair to you," I told her. "And I'm sorry for that—if that's what you mean by feeling sorry for you."

"What about my parents?" she demanded.

"I'm sorry about that," I told her. "But I'd be sorry just the same, no matter whose parents it was—yours or mine or anybody else's."

She looked really sad then. She just dropped all that guardedness.

"Every time I go to church, I think that everyone must be talking about us," she said. I realized that Annette was a lot more worried about what the people at church said or thought about her than I'd ever been. But, that was Annette.

"I think people there would like to help if they could," I told her. "But when all this happened here to us, none of our parents were around. If I like you and can be friends with you, it's because of you, not your folks. I think that Penny and Jean feel the same way," I added. "We can all be friends."

"And what about Scruggs?" she asked.

"He's got to speak for himself."

"Well, he did apologize to me yesterday," she said.

I privately still thought that Scruggs would have kept his mouth shut the whole way through about what he'd figured out, if Annette had just left him alone.

"I know what you're thinking," she said, "and I told him I was sorry, too." After a moment she added, "After all, he was right all along about what we had to do. I know when I've been wrong."

"Maybe everybody can be friends now," I said. I stood up. "After all, the Lord gives adventures, and this adventure came to all of us, and we're all Vikings now."

Just then the food came, and everybody else came back in.

Chapter Twenty-five
Viking Dropouts, All!

Our disappearance had made quite a stir, although the snow kept us isolated for a little while longer. We spent another day lying around and eating while the skies cleared and the roads were plowed.

Our folks and Uncle Bill ended up arriving at just about the same time. He got to Andover just a little bit ahead of them. His face looked really pale—almost gray, in fact. I think it hit all of us that our folks had been really worried about us. We'd been so worried about ourselves that we hadn't had a lot of time to concentrate on them.

The van had been recovered, and the things that we'd left behind were brought back to us. But the materials that Sam Vierowe and his partner had taken were gone forever. So, in fact, were Sam Vierowe and his partner. They were never traced.

Everybody else from Peabody came in that evening. Mom and Dad came, and Mrs. Bennett, and Annette's father. The reunion should have been a happy one for all of us. But Annette cried a lot harder than you'd think from a kid who was being safely returned after a long adventure. And her father cried. They walked out together into the snowy night, talking, but I knew she was crying as they went, and I thought that she sounded like she was begging him about something. I could have guessed what.

Penny hugged Mom and Dad really hard, and I knew what she was thinking. And Mom and Dad knew that we knew about it, but nobody said anything right then.

They got a cabin for themselves, and later, when Dad and I were alone, I asked him about it.

"Do you think that maybe now Annette's parents will stay together?"

He turned and looked at me. "Son, it's not our business to speculate about things like that. That's what the Bible calls idle talk." He had been rummaging in his suitcase looking for his razor.

"But I thought maybe this would have shocked them or something," I added.

"It shocked all of us," Dad told me. "But I can't say what Annette's folks have concluded from it. They've talked to your mother and me—very long and very seriously. But they have to go to the Lord Himself, and the Cross, to get the strength and grace to stay together and make things work."

"Well, we did," I told him. "Out on the trail. I think we all changed."

"Look," he told me, "Annette's parents are together for the moment. And we have to pray for them, and we have to pray for Annette. They all need grace, and they all need strength."

"Okay," I said.

"But I'm glad that you're all friends," he said. "We were praying for that, too."

The next day Annette and Penny spent a lot of time

talking with each other. I could see that they'd gotten to be pretty close friends. I think there was a time when I would have asked Penny what Annette had told her, but I didn't ask her then. Penny was always going to be my friend, but now we had other friends, too. And Penny seemed a lot older than she'd ever seemed before.

We weren't going to get to spend any time in Littleton. The vacation was over. We'd have to be in school on Monday.

"Nothing left but that awful plane ride back to Peabody," Scruggs said.

"At least our folks will be with us," Penny told him.

He grinned. "Yeah, maybe it won't be so bad with Mother scolding me about not trusting the Lord." Then he laughed. Penny laughed, too. It was hard to picture soft-spoken Mrs. Bennett scolding about anything.

Scruggs still had Lumberjax. He set it down on the breakfast table while we all hauled our luggage out. We had a three-hour drive to the airport, and Uncle Bill was coming to get everybody in a station wagon that he'd rented.

"Will they let you take Lumberjax on the plane?" Penny asked him. Annette and Jean came in, dragging their things.

"They'd better," Scruggs said. "We can't leave our sword behind!"

He held it up, and I put my hand on it.

"Vikings all?" he asked.

Jean and Penny took it too, and Scruggs looked at Annette. He held it out to her. She reached out and put her hand on it.

"I'll be Arwyn," she said softly.

"Hail, and well met," Scruggs told her. "Arwyn,

ABANDONED

Berwyn, Ooné, Leif, and Eric, Vikings all!"

"Viking dropouts, all!" Penny exclaimed.

Outside, a horn beeped for us. "There's the Viking ship! All aboard that's going aboard!" I said. We grabbed our stuff and headed for the door.